METAMORPHOSES
Stories She May Tell

"In some stories you read to me," Norma replies, "all is described so well: the streets of the town or the cities, the sidewalks, the parks, the traffic. In these places described so real, humans behave strangely. They behave erratically as if their minds are not present, as if they are not there. The inanimate subjects are real, but the humans are not. You have read me stories like that."

"Why don't you tell me a story?" Celeste asks and Norma answers:

"Maybe I will, maybe I will."

There is a twinkle in Norma's now wide-open eyes. Is Celeste detecting a promise?

--Excerpt from Metamorphoses: *Stories She May Tell*

Praise for
Metamorphoses

"In her new collection of short stories, <u>Metamorphoses</u>, Dr. Brisco continues to engage us with the emotional odysseys of a range of women who come, in ways memorable and trivial, to crossroads in their lives. As in <u>Women in Transition</u>, the music, elegance, and wit of her writing style continue to draw the reader into the worlds her characters inhabit. In <u>Metamorphoses</u>, however, Brisco takes even greater risks as an author, to move deeper into the souls of her protagonists. She puts us through their trials; she offers us their little and large epiphanies for our own. In short, <u>Metamorphoses</u> is an aesthetic and most satisfying read."

> Elaine Barden, PhD, Retired speech-language pathologist and faculty member, Department of Communication Sciences & Disorders, Montclair State University, Montclair, NJ

"Dr. Brisco's latest book deals with universal themes such as love, death, life's joys and disappointments, but never leave the trials and tribulations of everyday life far behind. With her distinct writing style, she captures the imagination of her readers and draws us into a world filled with a diverse cast of characters, all who unabashedly display their foibles and their triumphs before us. It is easy to become absorbed in reading each story and easier still to form an intimate relationship with the characters. These personalities are familiar and yet not so familiar – they are part of the embodiment of situations we may all have to cross in our own lives. A wonderful literary accomplishment."

Angela Meola, Assistant Director, The Center for Italian & Italian American Culture, Inc.

"In her second book, <u>Metamorphoses</u>, Margaret Brisco shares more than just personal stories, with simplicity that moves us to read one and than another and then another. She also shares observations gained by viewing her childhood through the lenses of years of experience sharpened with the understanding of human nature. Stories such as 'It is Only a Movie' open both the child and the reader up to questions of why the surface story needs to contain shadows of violence and hurt. A treasure of the book!"

Ethel Lee-Miller author of <u>Thinking of Miller Place: A Memoir ofSummer Comfort</u>

mbrisco329@comcast.net
Booklocker.com, Inc.

METAMORPHOSES
Stories She May Tell

Margaret Brisco

To Arlen a best wishes
Margaret Brisco
2009

Also by Dr. Margaret Brisco

Women in Transition (I am a Wanderer)

Childbirth: A Unique Experience

To Annamaria and Ralph
To Christen and Mark

ACKNOWLEDGEMENTS

I would like to acknowledge the following people who helped immensely with the publishing of this book:

My beloved daughter, Annamaria Stefanelli, and my dear friend, Elaine Barden, for being my editors and advisors,

To Write Group of Montclair, NJ, a group of writers who lent their experience and advice,

A special thank you to Angela, Ennette, Rose and Yolanda.

To all my friends, too numerous to mention, who never stopped believing in me and gave me courage and moral support, a million thanks. My accomplishment is their accomplishment.

And last, but not least, I am very grateful to my publicist, Marcia Mungenast. Her talents and capabilities are superb.

TABLE OF CONTENTS

Part I: Norma 1

The Stories She May Tell.................................... 3

A Month of February 9

The Promise of Spring 12

Dialogue 14

Letters.. 19

Leaving.. 27

Remembering Sunsets.............................. 34

It Is Only a Movie 35

A Story About Fish 37

The Story of Fish II 39

Her Father's Garden.............................. 42

Metamorphoses 44

Part II: Homes.. 47

Sleep.. 49

Homeless.. 52

Shredding 55

Visit.. 60

A Day in the Life of Maggy Brown 68

Part III: Other Stories 71

After the Fall 73

Remembering Laura.............................. 82

A Woman 88

It Could Be Worse.................................. 91

A Cat in the Corner 92

After The Fall II 94

Memory 100

Part IV: Norma **101**
Traveling Alone 103

Appendix...**119**

Part I: Norma

The Stories She May Tell

Celeste is plagued by a sense of guilt. Guilt, at being well off while others are suffering and being depraved. Or abandoned, forgotten, lonely.

Or being hungry.

She has never known hunger. Thick steaks, potatoes, side dishes of veggies. Broccoli - her favorite. Or pasta with different salsas on it. And in the morning, cereal with milk and coffee for grownups.

A housewife and a mother, what has she done with her life?

Does everyone have to do heroic deeds?

Her feelings of guilt have been developing over the years. She considers herself selfish, self-serving, remote. Wars have come and gone in front of her. Famine, diseases, the suffering of women in childbirth without help or hope. So many miseries, while she did her chores and pampered her children.

The children, now grown and educated, travel the world. It is incredible that with all the trouble in the world they travel to the most distant, "exotic" parts of it. Strange languages, strange cultures that they want to discover, to participate in and up to the certain point, to absorb. It would be difficult to absorb them completely. They are like the old Romans who said clearly, "civis romanus sum". They being Americans. Good or bad? Who knows? To use a "cliché, "time will tell."

Sometimes Celeste thinks that she is too harsh with herself. It is not her fault the world is upside down, topsy-turvy, while she has her comforts, her three or four course meals and her nice clothes. Yet, she feels guilty. She has to do something: "I have to give. To give some."

She so desired to offer her services to others. Which others? There are so many who need help. She chose the least difficult, the least dangerous. She chose to help an elderly woman with reading and conversation.

****

The elderly woman, Norma, lives in her own home, a rarity today, in a house that is old by modern standards. The walls are thick and the interior is full of shadows. Dark wood walls, a large wooden parquet floor. It certainly is not one of the "Mac mansions," the ones coming up these days like mushrooms after rainy days. Most in the same style, pretentious, possibly cheaply built. Crowded, close to each other. Will they last for a long time? Like the old ones? A friend of Celeste had once said: "The buildings of today are the slums of tomorrow." Possibly an exaggerated statement, but who knows?

Norma's kitchen is antiquated, but she does not cook much. No entertaining any more. Visits from family and good friends at times, with food delivered from outside.

Whenever Celeste walks into Norma's home, she finds her sitting in her overstuffed chair, with an afghan on her knees in winter and with no afghan in summer and fall. She reminds Celeste of the birds that survive the winter, or of the bear that sleeps through it. She is thin.

"Why don't you eat some meat?" Celeste inquires and Norma answers:

"There is so much violence in the world. I do not wish to contribute to the killing."

Books and papers are spread around the room in a haphazard manner. Celeste thinks that it is impossible for Norma at this point of her life to keep tabs on it at all. Celeste knows that the old lady is trying to keep certain categories separate: fiction, poetry, non fiction. But it is impossible for her to master this order of things. Instead, she categorizes accordingly, to the books that she loves and the ones she is indifferent about.

Never mind: she lives in this mess of paper and does not wish to be disturbed.

"I am above being concerned," she says wistfully, although Celeste knows she would like all things in order. Celeste cannot help her here: it is overwhelming. So she sits in a chair across from Norma and waits.

Norma is old. How old is she? Her face is an oval of wrinkles that with makeup does not appear that noticeable. She wears large bifocal glasses with dark frames -- "jazzy" as someone had said to her once. Celeste suspects that she hides her edematous eyelids behind those glasses. Her eyes look small in all that flesh.

"Once, I had beautiful eyes with long eyelashes" Norma has said. "Now they are not beautiful and do not serve me well. I do not remember their color. I think that they are green."

"Wishful thinking," Norma says again and giggles.

She has a wonderful sense of humor mixed with some melancholia, as if she is telling a story. She discusses her name using her humor:

"You should call me Madame Norma, but that would not be very appropriate. Someone may think that I ran a bordello in my young days. I am not Mrs. Norma or Miss Norma any more so calling me Norma is just fine. The American way.

Her garden is overgrown, but not abandoned. No grass to cut, no manicured lawn, but bushes and pebbles and some pachysandra under the trees. Bushes of forsythia and occasionally some flowers trying to survive. Tall trees keep shade in the summer. Oaks, maples and some lilacs.

This elderly woman who stays in the old house and does not wish to move into more comfortable quarters. A nursing home. Or an assisted living community.

She does not wish to live where the accommodations may be exceptionally good, with a proper dining room, exercise room, comfortable bedrooms. Possibly with a faint smell of urine. And the people you have become friendly with will be dying in front of your eyes. One at a time. Constantly, with the rhythm of the seasons. Only, there are no seasons: there is only the certainty of passing.

Norma uses the gentle word, "passing."

"I will pass in my own place, in my own rhythm," she tells Celeste. "I do not mind living alone. Sooner or later we all remain alone."

Celeste respects Norma's privacy. Actually, she admires it. She thinks: "Hopefully, I may imitate her or evoke her memory when my time comes. For me, still far away. And if Norma does not dwell on it, I surely will not."

In the newspapers, it is often written how so and so, famous politician, famous diva, famous actor or actress has died "peacefully" in their home. The home may be anywhere: big city, foreign country, or exotic lands. The very poor die also in their houses that may be in great disrepair, possibly falling apart, possibly full of dust, garbage and uneaten food. It comes to her that the very rich and the very poor have something in common. They do not have to worry where they may wind up when dead.

"Absurd, rich and poor the same?" Celeste thinks, and is ready to read to Norma from the New York Times. But the next time she will bring a book. A contemporary writer. She is sure the old one has read the classics.

****

At times Norma looks at Celeste and listens carefully to the reading, and at times Celeste sees her looking into the distance, her eyes semi-closed, her eyelids heavy over her eyes. Celeste interrupts the reading and asks if she liked the story.

"In some stories you read to me," Norma replies, "all is described so well: the streets of the town or the cities, the sidewalks, the parks, the traffic. In these places described so real, humans behave strangely. They behave erratically as if their minds are not present, as if they are not there. The inanimate subjects are real, but the humans are not. You have read me stories like that."

"Why don't you tell me a story?" Celeste asks and Norma answers:

"Maybe I will, maybe I will."

There is a twinkle in Norma's now wide-open eyes. Is Celeste detecting a promise?

As Norma says:

"These days, as I sit here and stare, the forgotten times come back to me in spurts. In flashes, memories come and go and some repeat themselves at the most inopportune times, most undesirable times. The forgotten comes back. I should be able to tell stories, although I have put them away long ago and do not look back for them. Some are like souvenirs, not disturbances. The spurts, the flashes. The forgotten stories. It is possible that they are not true, these stories that come to me in the middle of the night like lightning. And then go away. They could have happened anywhere in the world and perhaps to someone else. Strange memories come back and disturb my rest. I have forgotten most of them and never wanted to look back. It seems that it was in my nature to forget. And to look ahead."

Where does she come from? How long she has been collecting the memories?

Norma told Celeste once:

"I am going to bring all my old friends to this house. They can spend time with me as long as they wish. Weeks, months. I am talking of those who are alone. You can read to all of us."

She looked at Celeste quizzically as if waiting for her to complain. Or to refuse to do it. But Celeste just smiled. She envisioned all these women, full of wisdom, with a past that may be interesting, sad, tragic, hilarious or dark. They did survive: are they wise, are they smart or perhaps have they forgotten?

Celeste is waiting patiently for the many stories that Norma will tell.

A Month of February

A strange, misbehaving winter.

"Madness, sheer madness," Norma thinks, looking through the window into the winter scene. January was mild with temperatures that made it seem as if it were autumn. Then February came with severe cold and a cruel wind. She feels the cold although the house is warm with hot radiators. But it is eleven degrees outside and she feels the eleven degrees in her house that has the radiators steaming. She does not like winter. She wraps herself into an afghan with a scarf around her neck and a warm hat on her head.

Her nose is cold.

It reminds her of the cold nose of her mother's cat that, according to her mother, should be always cold. If the cat is healthy, the nose stays cold. That is mother's health observation of her cat.

"I am not a cat," Norma thinks and rubs her nose gently with her hands. Her hands are reasonably warmed. She had worn her gloves off and on most of the day.

Celeste is not coming today. The roads are icy and it is dangerous to drive.

Norma curiously opens the door that leads to the patio: the air is cold and clean. The sky above is gray, uniformly gray, looking solid with no transparency. But on the right there is a patch of blue, baby blue like her father's eyes were, with a streak of white slashing through the blue, cutting it in half. Its white makes the blue bluer. The blueness.

What makes the streak of white, cutting the blue in half as if with a knife?

Norma keeps returning to the window to look at the blue and white, because they are beautiful and promising. The promise of warmth and of spring.

The last time she went to look, they were not there any more.

It is February, it is winter.

Norma remembers another February, the one of her youth when it was also cold -- and the brisk, clean air that she did not fear. She would challenge the cold and walk through it, feeling purified by its cleanliness and its transparency.

When March comes, it is time to open the windows and let the smell of good earth come through.

Should she remember a cold March that did not keep its promise? The dark days of war. Does anybody remember still? Humans have short memories. They adjust. It is good to be able to adjust. The brain changes its synopsis and we start all over again. It is good to be able to start again. She walks through her house in silence. This is her cave, her own personal cave.

After a few days, the weather improves and Celeste comes to see her.

"Do you have enough food in the house?" Celeste asks and Norma smiles.

"I have enough to eat. I will not starve. It is good to see you. And how are you coping with this cold?"

"Oh, I am used to it," Celeste answers. " I like the change of seasons. It is winter and the mountains will be full of skiers, young and old."

Norma has nothing to say. She does not ski. She, for some reason, never did. But it is nice to have Celeste come and see her. They will sit and talk and Celeste will tell her what is going on in the world. Enough of silence, enough of cave.

Celeste will make a strong cup of coffee. It is good to have a cup of coffee. Decaffeinated.

Norma would like an eternal spring or even better, an eternal autumn. She sits with Celeste, sips her coffee and thinks of March coming.

The Promise of Spring

How many times has the promise come and gone? How many times have we lost it? Memory is failing. It refuses to remember. Too many lost springs.

And yet, whenever spring comes it is always like the beginning. The beginning of something new. Forgetting the past ones and the shortness of it. Forgetting that it will not last.

After spring the hot summer will come, burning our skins, making our eyes tear. We will hide in the cold rooms, or jump into the water, or we will sun ourselves nude on the rocks next to the sea, like many lizards who would lay immobile only changing their moods and their colors.

But at present the spring is here and the breeze is like a healing ritual in some ancient church. The trees are talking to us with their green leaves, and the flowering ones are sending their aromas toward us. And we live and we breathe and we love again among the colors the perfumes and the breezes.

We greet each other and talk freely and laugh aloud in the promise of spring.

The promise of many lost springs. But are they really lost or do they live and they survive in our souls in our own conquests and defeats or our own solitudes? And with the aromas, the breezes and the color of flowers.

<u>Epilogue</u>
And the poem by Anna:
"I search again;
the beginning is much like the end;
meanings fall like blades of grass;
freshly cut they pretend it is spring again;
I face the wall;
the meanings fall, again."

Dialogue

Leaving her friend's house on the corner of the quiet street in the town of Bloomfield. Modest homes, neat, with small patches of grass in front, some bushes, some flowers. Peaceful.

She had a good visit with her friends, with talks of books they had recently read, travels, the birthdays of children.

Feeling good and accomplished, she opens the door of her car to get in, her pocketbook on her left arm. Another car is turning the corner, fast, as in a hurry: a silver Toyota Corolla, four-seater. The car stops next to her and a young man jumps out of it and runs toward her. He is young, with a bouncy graceful walk, almost a dance. He runs toward her and yells, "Hi lady." She looks at him and perhaps is smiling. She thinks that he may need direction or perhaps may wish to park in the spot she is just going to leave. He comes close, and quickly and skillfully snatches the pocketbook off her left arm.

She is trying to stop him and she yells, "oh no no, no" as if totally disappointed in him. In his behavior. But he is stronger than she is. He pulls the purse away and runs into the Toyota, and the car takes off, fast toward the avenue. She is stunned: nothing like this has ever happened to her.

Closing her car door, she runs into her friend's house and tells them what has happened.

They are very upset. They make her sit down and give her a glass of water then call the police to report the theft. They are upset. Things like this should not happen on this quiet street.

She feels strange, as if this has not happened to her, that all the hassle is about some other person, not her sitting quietly on the chair and taking sips of water from an offered glass. She is repeating the scene in her mind, not believing it, seeing the smiling face of this young man, so young, so bouncy, so athletic. Why did he do it? She had trusted him, and wanted to tell him how to go where he wanted. Skillfully, he pulled the pocketbook off her arm, without hurting her. Without breaking her arm. Or her skull.

****

Two policemen came into the friend's home, one short and fat, the other tall with a smooth face and pensive eyes looking at her. They took notes, but she could not tell them much. The car was shiny, new. She remembered the double insignia of the Toyota and the word Corolla but she couldn't remember the license plate.

"Don't worry about it," the fat policeman said, "It is probably stolen." They took the description of the car and the young man. There were others in the car, not very visible, only shadows.

There were personal objects in that pocketbook. Besides the credit cards, cell phone and glasses, her business cards were there with her address, her worldly titles, the phone numbers, her email address. Will he call? Will he be apologetic, insulting, rude?

Having spent the rest of the day in the house canceling the credit cards and changing the door locks, she was starting to feel afraid. A vague feeling of danger.

In the late afternoon, the phone rang. She answered as usual, thinking that perhaps her friends were calling to check on her. A policeman was on the phone.

"Your pocketbook was found" he said, "You can come and retrieve it. Bring some identification."

"My pocketbook? Where it was found?" she asked, not quite believing.

"On the corner of a street not too far from where it was stolen. A crossing guard brought it to the station. By the way, everything is inside."

"My credit cards?"

"Your credit cards and your driver's license"

She could not believe it.

She felt weak, not able to go to the police station.

"Can you bring it to me?" she asked, sounding tired, sick, deflated.

Did the police officer sense her weakness, her emotional fatigue? The sergeant came to the phone: "I will bring it to you later in the afternoon, Ma'am."

In the evening, the sergeant from the detective bureau brought the pocketbook to her home. He seemed to be very pleased to be able to do it. He smiled and his blue eyes were sparkling. Sitting in her living room they examined the contents of the pocketbook.

She was surprised how "untouched" it appeared. The inside was neat and orderly as if nothing had happened to it. Her favorite scarf was there neatly folded, her credit cards, driver's license were there. Her cell phone and sunglasses were missing. So was a small amount of cash that she had in the purse. Were they angry because of the small amount of cash they found? Everything was so orderly.

She opened a small compartment in her purse. In it, she kept few souvenirs, and a copy of a *retablo.* "Nuestra Senora de Guadalupe." A souvenir from Santa Fe. The retablo was made the same way the santeros were making it since the sixteen-century. Why did he take it, he and his friends in the back seat of the stolen Toyota? Did the picture tell him something? The pocketbook was clean and neat, not violated.

****

He has her phone number and she is waiting for him to call her. She would thank him for not being destructive and defiling. For leaving her beautiful scarf neatly folded inside with the rest of her possessions. She imagines that he is calling her perhaps to taunt her and perhaps not. He is on the phone or she would like it to be so, and she hears his mocking voice:

"Hi, lady!"

"It is you," she says "I was waiting for your call."

"Is that so?" The voice is clear with no special accent, no patois.

"I wanted to thank you for not destroying my property. My scarf was still there, clean and neatly folded."

"I took your money," he insists.

"There was not much money. And the cell phone can be replaced," she adds.

There is a pause.

"It was a prank," he says slowly.

"You took my picture of the Madonna. What is your background? Your race?" She adds tentatively.

"Human race," mockingly again. "Unfortunately," he adds in a slow voice.

"Do you have a family?" she asks, and he replies:

"Not much. Would you like to adopt me?"

"I can't do that," she says.

"Words, words, words," he quotes Shakespeare although she is sure he never read him.

"I know," she says, "I am a failure."

He laughs. The laughter is between the amused and the cynical. He says:

"Well, goodbye, my lady."

"Please call again," she says.

He hangs up and there is a silence. She hopes that he will call again.

Perhaps he will give the icon to his grandmother. "La nuesta Senora De Guadalupe."

Letters

My dear Friend,

I have been following you from a distance. I wonder: how does it feel to live between two worlds and fly like a bird from one place to another?

You and I left each other long time ago. Left with harsh words. Each of us thought that the other was unreasonable, opinionated, and tried to tell the other how to live. Thinking of it now, I find it so insignificant and trite. I think now that it all was laughable at best.

But we were young, intolerant, brash. And insecure. We could not forgive each other our small mistakes, peculiarities, idiosyncrasies. So we became, if not enemies, certainly full of animosities toward each other. Never to see each other again.

What a loss.

I live in a small house, on top of a hill, with trees that grow wild around it and other small houses that are at some distance from each other. A road meanders between the trees and the homes. Up the hill, nature rages whenever it has the occasion. The wind is strong and blows a lot even when the city is relatively calm. The rains are profuse and when the fog comes it is thick and impenetrable. Driving through it, one feels that there may be nothing else but the fog. It is all so encompassing. I love to drive through it and feel that I perhaps am not of this world.

When I slowly move down the hill and into the town, everyday reality comes to meet me. I become an everyday person again.

An average person.

Running small chores. Getting small acquisitions.

At present, I live alone. The children live elsewhere, but close enough for me to see them relatively often.

After two marriages (disastrous), and a few male friends (inconsequential), I am alone in the small house on the hill, where Mother Nature is a noisy neighbor and the fog brings me into another dimension (or so I feel).

I think that, perhaps, some women are meant to be alone. Predestined.

I have broken this rule and tempted the gods twice and each time it was unsuccessful. But not totally. There are the children. Children no more. They kid themselves that I am strong and eternal. It is easier that way. We are all relatively at ease, at peace.

It is winter now and the trees fascinate me. I like them in summer when they are full of foliage, but in winter I watch them -- tall, bare, vulnerable yet threatening. Stretching their branches up to heaven. The heaven in winter is not blue but gray, covered with clouds. Sometime in the evening, when the winter sun goes down on the horizon, the clouds are purple. Dark purple. With pink sunny borders and a light of their own. It is the best part of the day. We still get the sun occasionally and when we do if nature is still with no rain or snow falling to obscure the horizon, the sun will peek out on the east and the sky will be all blood red.

This is my world in winter.

Is summer coming?

As I speak of women alone, I see that you never got married. I heard vague rumors that you and your boss are lovers, but I do not believe it. I wonder whether you are still celibate, still "Virgo intacta". Anatomically or spiritually. Who knows?

While I sit in my chambers on the hill in the small house, scribbling my reports and short stories, you are moving between your two worlds, your two planets. Traveling, catching airplanes. Being a bird and crossing oceans.

I have seen your picture in the newspapers. You, the great benefactor of important causes. I was surprised to see a fat old lady with small beaded eyes imbedded in fat. Or was it just your heavy eyelids and bags under your eyes? You surely have gained some weight. But then I was thinking that my photograph may have a similar impression on you. I am not young anymore and my thin face is covered with very fine wrinkles.

I surely miss your blue eyes; they were the best part of your features, the only beautiful part of you. (If I may say so with a touch of malevolence). I loved your blue eyes. Why did you bury them in layers of fat?

You may think that I am old, crotchety and cruel. Or, it may occur to you to think that I may be envious of your worldly successes.

Who knows? It is possible that I may be envious, but I do not think so. I think that I am just honest. But who can tell what is hidden under the surface of our persona, after so many years of living?

I am going to terminate this script, not knowing whether I will or will not mail it to you. Your personal address is unknown to me, but in the institution that you serve (or that serves you) it would be easy to find you and deliver it.

I will write to you again whether it is going to be forwarded or not.

We will see.

Your old friend who remembers

****

My dear Friend,

Here I am writing to you again. Since I do not have a steady job, I have time to think and to remember.

I am following, in thoughts, my old friends, long lost and, for a time, forgotten, to revive them in my memory and thus to see the changes in myself. Are these letters for you, or is this a memoir to myself? You decide.

I am not disappointed in myself. I look at you and others through myself and I am not disappointed. It seems that I have been a long time living. But then, it seems as if I have still much to accomplish in front of me. Is this a contradiction? I sit and write in the silence of my various rooms, in which are dispersed various books and manuscripts. At these times, I like my aloneness. At other times, I am with my children. Then there are my friends. All different and yet similar in their creative femininity. It is good to share.

Do you miss not having children? I am sure that you have other satisfactions. Is it hard to find yourself alone after all the ceremonies, feasting, and presentations? But then, I should not talk since I myself am also alone. Because I know how it is to be alone.

I understand that you recently visited our old haunts. I was thinking of the sun and of the fresh air streaming inside the open balconies from the sea. The sailboats would be docked at the inlet that extends itself from the water into the land like a large benign serpent. I also plan to visit in summer. Or spring. It will be hot and I would need to go into the water to become a fish again. I would like to drift into the sacred island on the lagoon. We used to go there often. Remember?

Your long lost friend

P.S. When we were still friends and you would travel to visit home or to various seminars, before boarding the airplane you would go swimming. You would arrive at the plane still in your swimming suite with just a summer dress over it. You loved water.

Where I live now, the summers are hot and humid. But the springs are full of flowers, foliage and beauty. Then, when summer comes, people run to the waters and some sun themselves like lizards stretched out on the sand and the jetties. Some hide from the sun in the shades of the umbrellas in order to protect their skins.

Do you still catch airplanes in your swimming suit? I doubt it. You must be much more if not sedentary certainly more laid back. It would be hard for you to be impulsive in your refined world of research and acquisitions.

(I also understand the unpleasantness of exposing our twisted bodies with their folds of flesh positioned in wrong places.)

So be it. Not to care.

I think that it is still beautiful to worship the sun, in summer when there is not too much shade to find, and bodies sweat and burn. To be embraced by its rays.

Let it be light.

****

Dear Friend,

When I watch the horizon in summer, distended on the secluded beach and forgetting the sun's dangers, my eyes may wander and I may imagine the white passenger ships passing slowly by. The ones that my parents took on their voyage to foreign countries. Vulcania. Saturnia. The "Ille De France," a picture of the great ship, hung in the corridor of our house. But it is not there anymore. To where did it disappear?

I do not know. Nothing is the same. And yet…

Take care. I hope that you are happy.

Your friend

P.S.   I have found out from the newspapers that you have retired from your very preeminent job. With great pomp and many rewards. Talks about your capacity, generosity and altruism were abundant. You have also received a plaque, which will hang in the great hall with your picture and a dedication.

It must have been a great satisfaction to you. A pleasure, a pride.

Are you going to enjoy your retirement? Or will it be a bittersweet realization that the others now will be taking your place and will continue the work that you started? And that you may fade after a while into the background and slowly disappear?

Perhaps the plaque with your picture will eventually be removed and someone else's picture will be put in its place? Perhaps your young colleagues would have a sigh of relief that you have faded away and left room for their achievements and their successes?

"Tutto passa."

But perhaps, I am an old dinosaur sitting in my little house on the hill watching the world passing by. Perhaps I am being somewhat cynical, somewhat pessimistic, or even possibly a little bit jealous. Whatever it is, I remember the days of our traipsing through our little universe, walking through the narrow streets of the ancient university town. And you jumping in the water at the end of school semester, and getting on the plane in a wet swimsuit under your summer dress.

I smile and remember.

I hope that your days are bright and joyous and that you would still jump in the sea and get salty and wet.

This will be the last letter from

Your old friend

Answer to the previous letter:

Dear long lost friend,

Your letter has reached me (I understand there have been a few) while I was attending a scrumptious banquet where I was a celebrated person and where many "brindisi" (toasts) were offered in my honor. (Ha, ha, ha.)

Are you impressed?

It does seem to me that you are somewhat envious of my successes in the world of our industrious culture. You seem to know a lot about me while I know so little about you.

Please do not be envious. My life has been a straight line of hard work, long hours of seclusion and research. And as everything in life, in spite of the articles in the journals and the newspapers it is just effort, effort, effort.

I do not want to sound depressed, tired or jaded. I am not. I am what I am, and at the moment of my retirement I am looking back at the years with a certain amount of pleasure and satisfaction.

Life is not a string of colorful jewels or feasting in corporate rooms with crystal challises, and Veuve Clicot champagne. Where is the work? Where are the hotel rooms in which, deadly tired from "crossing the world," as you so picturesquely describe, we fall in cold hotel beds?

Now I am exaggerating. I am fine. There is a lot of satisfaction. And it is possible that I also may have a spot of envy on my part for your fog and the wild flora. And the children who, however occasionally, find time to keep you company in your modest home on the hill.

I do not have your picture. I do imagine you still slim, not bent by osteoporosis. Still having a great pair of legs, but a scanty, thin, miserable set of hair on your head. Why don't you cut it short, very short, so that your features are exposed, with all the fine wrinkles across your face?

As you see, I can be at times as malevolent as you can.

I do remember our friendship although it has sunk into the distance of years of work and perseverance. It comes back to me when I fly back home during vacation time and brings me back into the youth.

Why did we have to be so unforgiving with each other? Perhaps our lives would have been different. My blue eyes would not have been hidden in layers of hanging skin folds. And, you instead of being overly thin would have gained a few pounds.

Who knows?

It was nice to hear from you. It is possible that by accident we may meet again, older and wiser on the shore of the Adriatic. And like old sages, will be able to laugh together and have fun.

All my best to you

Your old friend

P.S. My boss being my lover? That remains a question mark for you to ponder.

Leaving

"To leave, it is like dying a bit". And yet, she did leave.

After that, they had just letters to share. It was hopeless, although they pretended that it was only temporary. She knew that she would not return. Returning is like losing a battle, like losing the whole war. And yet, she kept the illusion, not out of hypocrisy or for lying, but because even to her it was something that could not be forgotten.

The letters kept coming.

She waited for their arrival. They were like an anchor in the world where she was still a stranger. After reading his letters, she would fantasize sometimes that walking down a strange street she would meet him and they would recognize each other, even after a period of time. And they would talk, laugh, reminisce or maybe they would cry.

"I walk the streets and think of you. I think that I will meet you there. I look at women who may look like you. My heart, why did you go away?"

So he once wrote.

She imagined herself similar to the immigrants who came to Ellis Island and expected a world of beauty and abundance, of peace and friendship. But it was not so. It was hardship, the reality of life to which they eventually adjusted themselves over time to became a part of the whole.

She did not come to Ellis Island. She came on a passenger ship and had a degree. Could she have stayed in the country to which she was adjusted, to which she belonged culturally and emotionally? Should she have stayed with him in spite of all, since they were made for each other? They shared everything: studies, food, bed. They were like one.

And then, she left.

Good old Europe. How much we wanted to abandon her . After the war. It seemed that America was the place of progress, success, creativity and freedom and of all other wonderful qualities.

She was so young then.

"Restless" or "unstable." Depending on the mood she was in, she would call herself that. When she liked herself she would consider herself restless. And if she disliked herself she considered herself as unstable. Perhaps such is life: the contradiction of it.

And then, all they had were the letters. How could one live just by written words? They slowly sank into oblivion and became other people.

The letters remained.

After so many years she found those letters. Finding them, reminded her of her past life, of the past times she had abandoned so completely with only an occasional look back. She was older now, with a profession, a home and children. It was all structured in a proper and in a conventional way.

Should she read the letters?

If she had been younger, she probably would not have hesitated. Reading them would revive an episode, perhaps with appreciation or with some poetic curiosity and then she would be on her way, not thinking much about it. But it would be different now, as she was older, not so restless anymore and no longer "unstable".

Would it disturb her? She decided to wait for some time and then take a look.

She would wait for some time: for inspiration, for curiosity, for something else?

For remembrance.

There were times when she had desperately wanted to be like everyone else. To find a man, to be courted, to marry and live happily ever after. But that wish would not last for long. The challenge. The calling of the unknown. The irresistible wish to wander. Had it been worth it?

After years of forgetting, years filled with others, not remembering or thinking of it, she had found the letters.

Alone in her home, she had found the letters.

She did not know whether she should read it. It was like exhuming the body of someone long dead and reliving the life and the death of that person. She had no knowledge where and how he had disappeared from her life. Eventually no letters arrived any more.

Sitting in her comfortable chair she wondered. Would it be pleasurable to remember? Or would she feel a loss, a sorrow or perhaps a guilt? It made her think that eventually we all leave, one way or another. Slowly, sometimes cruelly.

In our mortal lives.

"Partir c'est mourir un peu,
    c'est mourir a ce qu'on aime. "

The first letter:

"It is spring. The spring that was to be ours but it is not. Green, yellow, multicolored spring that sings with the sounds of light. But it is distant and foreign, like those who should be close to us in order that we may feel the warmth and the beauty, of these spring days."

She thinks: "What is pushing us, what makes us, in spite of everything, in spite of all that we love, all that we are, what makes us leave, leave, leave for good and makes us lie to ourselves that we shall return?

His letter:

"I often walk by the house in which you used to live, and look up to your window. But there is no light there: your window is dark, your window does not say anything. Behind that window, there is a room in which we sat together, talked, belonged. Belonging. Had things that belonged to us, our things, We smoked, laughed,

and fought sometime. We drank strong espresso coffee or tea with no sugar. There we were happy. We were ourselves. The way we were. So, even today, those good happy days still live with us.

It is raining. Time is passing us by. Time is filled with waiting, boredom, it is ill with memories and hopes and wishes. The passing of time.

Days of spring, the summer days, then days of autumn and winter, the days when leaves are falling and walking becomes soft and noiseless. But then, when leaves are wet with rain, walking over them makes a swishing, loud and wonderful noise.

Remember?"

It is hard to understand why we abandon certain people. She was looking for reasons, trying to find a rational cause for such behaviors. It would seem that all is wonderful, passionate, total. That life is ours and that we share the beauty of it, feeling deeply the heartbeats of life.

And then we leave.

They were so complete with each other. So totally. When she thinks of it, it has seemed so impossible that two people could be so completely attuned.

And then one leaves.

She cannot read any more: One should never look back. Looking back, the life energy starts failing us, and the days become somber and difficult. An emptiness should be created in place of memories and old songs. Into this emptiness instead we put new contents and new songs.

New happiness, new lives.

It is hard to live. If one remembers. Let's not remember. We all went our own ways, we all became Other.

"It is a warm summer night. Windy and warm. Sirocco. I am listening to the sea, to the melody of waves. I am listening and I remember: it is the way I would listen to the beating of your heart.

My sweet, my sweet."

I wish to write about everyday matters: my work my friends. But I cannot. I am sad, and if I write to you about my feelings and myself I would make myself even sadder.

Life is strange: in this moment I am sending you a thousand greetings and the moment is sacred, full of the need to live and to love. The yearning is so strong and it grows, like a tall tree that grows toward the blue of the sky."

She feels that a healing process has started. His healing process. And it will continue until there is no more room for the times of poetry, passion and the exquisite loving of youth.

The last ones: (letters).

"Your life lives in me. It navigates inside me like a vessel, a ship that is connecting our two words. You know how I loved you in those late evenings of tea and music.

When you left, with you were traveling my tears. You will always exist in all the places where I will ever live. Nothing can destroy the joy of my thoughts about you. In my world of happenings, you are a beautiful, a most beautiful and a most important memory. You live: you have to know this.

It is a New Year and a bit of old warmth for yours and my heart: I wish it for both of us."

The last sweet letters of good-bye. Sweet, touching letters.
So be it.

"...and we live our days, and a new sun, a new season of sun, wind, rains and the murmur of the sea.

I wish you happiness.

Whatever happens to us, I will always love you. As I did when we were together in winter, through fog and rain and always believing that the sun will come through."

Two years of waiting, two years of not knowing, two years of sweet hell,

and then a healing for him.

And for her, knowing that it had ended, the hemorrhaging and then bleeding slowly till it stopped.

Then it was all forgotten. Or was it? Such inconsistency. It was she who had left. But in the end it was he who left her for good.

Yes, she also wrote letters. Poetic, full of miseries and the terror of the loss. She is sure that those were eventually destroyed by him. Or perhaps by another woman.

"We make our own bed and we sleep in it."

Partir c'est mourir un peu,
C'est mourir à ce qu'on aime
On laisse un peu de soi-même
En toute heure et dans tout lieu.

Et l'on part, et c'est un jeu
Et jusqu'à l'adieu suprême
C'est son âme que l'on sème
Que l'on sème à chaque adieu

Partir, c'est mourir un peu

-- Edward Haracourt (1891)

Remembering Sunsets

The sunsets that she observed as young woman, while sitting on her patio, were always blood red. Looking into the distance when the sun would be setting behind the horizon, the air was clean, crisp and full of promises.

She would always remember: the color, the light and the sun nodding its goodbye at the end of the day.

The redness of the summer with the dreams of the beaches and the sands, and the nude bodies.

And she would remember the blood-red sunrises that would promise a coming of the clear day with no rains or heavy winds and no bad weather for that day. Now, sitting in her chair in the house, she remembers the reds.

The color of red.

She watches the television these days and the redness is that of blood that is spilled on the streets, on the beaches, the war fields, and the people's homes. The red blood of women and children, the old and the young, all bleeding their lives. Bleeding the country and bleeding the world. Blood, thick, viscous, collecting in pools and clotting away while the sun will appear again on the horizon, looking at the world and then hiding slowly behind it. It will return back in the early morning to leave the traces of its beauty, carrying its redness and watching humans bleed.

It Is Only a Movie

When I was a little girl, nine or ten years old, or perhaps even younger, my aunt would take me to the movies. She would choose a movie appropriate for a child, or so she thought. I was always looking forward to this day, going to the movies, because I liked her and liked to go out with her.

She would take me on holidays into the countryside with her friend, Esmeralda. "Esmeralda," that was her name. To me, it always represented the green of the emerald stone. And I would look at her whenever I could, trying to find the green light of the stone on her person -- her face, her eyes, her neck.

I remember that she used a lorgnon. Growing up, I would dream of being beautiful and having a lorgnon so I could look through it and see the world. No one ever knew that I had a fantasy about the green emerald and the lorgnon.

Young children live in a world of their own. And the grownups do not even dream that a child's world is a special world. Children keep their world within themselves as long as they can. And then, slowly, they become grownups. Only occasionally do they remember the reality of their childhood dreams.

Esmeralda, a beautiful, green emerald.

Esmeralda had a daughter who was my age. Her name was Velleda and the two of us would run around, stepping into the mud on the side of the roads, our shoes and sometimes our faces dirty, our clothing disheveled. My aunt would complain and she and Esmeralda would try to calm us down, but I knew they enjoyed that we were having a good time.

The movies were another story. As much as I looked forward to going out with my aunt, I also dreaded those movies with Stan and Olio, which I found violent and at times almost brutal. Olio was always hitting Stan, pushing him around, since Stan would always do something silly.

Poor Stan. I would cringe when Olio would hit him. Sometimes I would close my eyes not to look, hiding my discomfort from my aunt, because perhaps then she would not want to take me out again to the movies.

To her, it was only a movie.

For me, it was a painful experience, but I did not let her know that. I never said that they were cruel: all that hitting and pushing. Everybody in the theater would laugh, including my aunt. It was a funny movie, a movie for children.

Why are the movies for children always full of violence?

Snow-white and the seven dwarfs?

The Sleeping Beauty?

And the movies with Stan and Olio.

Are they trying to tell us something? To teach us about the world so that when we grow up we may be prepared?

Growing up, we forget the pushing, the smacking, the bullying. We do our own smacking and bullying and sometimes we get away with it.

And sometimes we don't.

Sometimes we accept the hurt and the violence. And sometimes we don't.

A Story About Fish

I remember two little gold fish that I had in a crystal bowl on the shelf in our parlor. I was four years old and I wanted a pet. Mommy did not like four-legged animals. Actually, she did not like pets at all. This is why I was given two gold fish in a reasonably large crystal bowl that was put on the shelf in the parlor. Each day, they were fed a special fish food and the water in the bowl was changed. I loved my fish and spent a long time watching them swim through the water. They seemed so happy.

Then one morning they were not swimming at all, and they were not moving. I was told that they had died and that mummy will "dispose of them."

Dispose of them? What did that mean?

"No, no, no," I cried and cried and mommy said that we would send them away.

And the next morning they were not there.

"Sent away? With angels?"

Mommy was an old-fashioned lady and children were to listen and not ask too many questions. It took me a long time to forget. No more gold fish. Their lives were too short. It was not good for them to be kept on the mantelpiece, no matter how often we changed the water and fed them fish food.

Years later, older and a mother, while visiting a sunny island in the Adriatic up north between Venice and Trieste, my son and I are sitting in the restaurant and we ask for fish.

A waiter brings two fish on a tray for us to see. He wants us to ascertain their freshness. An "orata" and a "branzino" lay there on the tray, their skins glistening, gray not gold. The eyes are open, not moving, not seeing.

I think:

Why will I eat you, you beautiful creature, that was swimming in the depths of the blue Adriatic water?

The fish does not answer.

The waiter takes the fish to the kitchen. Soon, we will be eating the fish.

I remember the Indian Nation, hunting buffalos, and with great respect thanking the buffalos for sacrificing themselves in order that the people might survive.

So I say in my thoughts to the fish that I am going to eat:

"Thank you for feeding me, my beautiful fish."

The fish does not answer.

The Story of Fish II

She is observing the jetty that has been beaten by the waves. The ocean is restless. The tide is high, trying to encompass the jetty and to submerge it . To make it its own.

The eternal fight between the land and the sea, the two giants who do not rest. The sea is angry and big waves are rising and traveling to the sandy beach. The same desire of the sea, the same persistence – to conquer the beach.

Then there is the jetty, almost covered with waves. The waves continue to claim the jetty, wishing to immerse it completely but not succeeding. Today the sea is not the winner; the jetty is.

Fishermen are standing on the jetty, casting their fishing lines into the water and not catching any fish. But they are patient and they continue their attempt at fishing. It is possible that eventually they may catch some. If they catch a reasonably big fish -- a striped bass, a fluke, or a blue fish -- they will bring it home and grill it on the outdoor grill in front of the old building where she used to live, making everyone envious. If only small fish are caught, they will throw them back into the ocean. Are the little fish still alive? Could the little fish swim away or will they die because of a fishhook that has torn their gills and their mouths? It seems that nobody thinks about the little fish. They have died in vain, not even being capable to feed the family of the fisherman, the one who owns the fish hook which tore into the fish's mouth and the fish's gills.

In the water the little fish will float for a while – and then, the little fish will be dead.

Let's not think about that.

There are surfers in the water trying to conquer the waves. Every so often "the big one" arrives and they glide on top of it on their surfboards, like big human birds, only to fall back into the water waiting for another big wave, waiting patiently. The water aficionados, the water creatures.

She wonders if in their past lives the aficionados perhaps were the small fish who the fishermen threw back into the ocean to die. Or perhaps they were the big ones grilled on the outdoor grills and eaten up by the humans. In their new lives they are surfers, waiting for the big waves, sailing on them, flying on them, and then falling back into the water from where they came.

She sits, peacefully, on the rattan chair on the lawn, high above the sandy beach and the jetty. Behind her is the old house with the red tiled roof, the narrow windows and lintels in need of constant repair.

The ocean is vast, the ocean is powerful. It scares her sometimes and she does not walk too close on the sandy beach. Did she drown in it in her past life? The sense of fear and the attraction that she feels for the sea. Wherever she goes she somehow always finds herself close to it.

She inhales the clean, salty air. She is going to sit there for a while, waiting for her friend to come.

Her friend finally arrives, breaking her silence, interrupting her thoughts.

"I thought you would be indoors," he says. "Are you cold?"

The sun is slowly disappearing, as if sneaking away, not to disturb. The fishermen are leaving the jetty. They are too far from her to see if they have caught any fish but their walk is light and she does not think they have caught any. It is silly but it makes her feel good. Here at the edge of the water there should be no mayhem.

Her friend sits next to her for a moment and observes the horizon.

"It is peaceful," he says, and adds, "Not too many people sit here and observe the moving of the ocean."

He knows that she has been waiting some time for him to come since they are to go to dinner together. "I am sorry that I am late," he says.

"No need for an apology, I have enjoyed sitting next to the ocean."

"With a bit of a distance," he teases, "Up on the higher ground."

"I love it here high," she says and he adds jokingly, "Perhaps you were a sailor once."

She looks at him and thinks: "Perhaps this is why I fear the sea. How does he know?"

"Let's go to dinner," she adds, and they walk to his car, parked on the side of the road.

"Where do we want to go?" she asks, and he answers, "Let's go to *Neal's*. It is next to the water."

Neal's, the restaurant, sits on the beach where, in the daytime, bathers come to swim, children build sandcastles and the sun worshippers worship the sun. It is a shallow beach and the water is much calmer than that on the jetty.

They drive there for dinner and he asks her, "Would you like to have fish for dinner?"

She thinks: "Was I a sailor or a fisherman? Or was I a fish, perhaps?"

She is confused: fisherman sailor, or fish?

"Yes, that would be nice," she says, "I will have salmon. Not home bred salmon. Or crabs."

He parks the car and they walk into the restaurant. They will eat fish.

Her Father's Garden

"To please or not to please."

He certainly liked his garden and watered it regularly, every evening when the sun would set. His garden, full of string beans, tomato plants, cauliflowers.

Was it a garden or a vegetable patch? It was too large to be called a vegetable patch.

We called it a garden. Mother's flowerbeds surrounded it. Mother also planted zinnias along the pathway that led to the house. It was grandfather's old house, that father kept and we all lived in it.

Why did he keep the old house that needed repairs? She did not know. She was only a child then, an innocent ten years old, wanting to please.

In front of the house were the trees: Peach trees, cherry trees and mulberry trees. The trees hid the house so that there was privacy and shade to protect the house and the garden from the scorching midday sun. The trees were very important to father.

How she wanted to please him, wanted for him to recognize her, to see her and to compliment her perhaps. So she chose to water the trees in front of the house every evening.

At the time when the sun would set, father would admire his garden, water his vegetable plants and mother's flowers and next to him she would be, with a large watering can in her hands, watering the trees.

One had to water the trees. The trees needed water.

Did he appreciate it? She was only a girl. A female.

She chose to water the trees in front of the house every evening. At the time when the Sun would set, father would admire his garden and water his vegetable plants, she would stand next to him with a special watering can in her hands and water the trees.

Every evening.

She was only ten years old. One had to water the trees.

Did he appreciate it? She was only a girl. A female.

Metamorphoses

Her friend Celeste was leaving for few weeks on a trip to Florida. It is winter. Being in Florida would be nicer and more comfortable than wrapping herself in an old afghan. But Norma really does not care.

Celeste is going to Florida.

Celeste is taking her grown up children with her. (Or are her children taking her?) This way they will be avoiding the cold weather, and possibly even snow, up north.

Celeste has made a feeble effort to invite Norma to come with them to Florida. It was not a real invite. Just a suggestion that Norma gracefully declined.

"What would Celeste do with one strange old lady on vacation, when she has her children with her?" Norma thinks.

Norma thinks and remembers.

She remembers the years when her home was full of people. Her own relatives: her mom and dad, her brother and sister. And always someone visiting and then staying apparently forever.

It was a great home. But was it a loving home? She was never sure. Mom never did much of anything, and father was of few words. Her family was the last one of their descendants. The last one. It was as if she had turned around and suddenly, no one was there. No close family, no cousins, and no distant relatives.

Why some families, she wonders, after years of prosperity, progress, perhaps abundance and increasing numbers, start to slowly to disappear? One by one, slowly and relentlessly, until only few are left.

She enjoys her friends, whom she sees occasionally, and with whom she goes out to lunch, to museums, and sometimes to the movies. She talks to them about books, politics, and weather.

Most of the weekends she is alone, since her friends may be visiting their own families, the grandchildren or some distant relatives.

Celeste is always concerned.

Nice person, nice lady.

Always the same questions:

"Do you have enough food in the house? Is it warm enough in your house?"

And advice:

"If it is icy do not go on the patio."

Norma nods her head as always and answers:

"Not to worry, I am good. I have everything"

Celeste promises to send her a card from Florida.

"Please do. I love to receive mail."

And it is true. Nowadays only advertisements arrive in the mail, trumpeting great deals or asking for donations. It is good to find, among all that mess, a friendly card, a letter and a note.

She looks for mail every day. She actually waits for it. Possibly just a habit from old times, or from being lonely. Someone may remember.

Her family had died out over a period of time. Actually, over a span of two centuries as far as she knows. There were stories of families with many children. Of the ones who left and went elsewhere. Some returning back and some remaining far away. Some writing notes to each other and sending photos of wives and children, the houses and the cars. And some disappearing never to be heard from again. The one distant, surviving cousin lives by herself, reads books and cooks gourmet meals for herself. Small meals, since she lives alone and has no family to feed. And the loved ones dying in distant places that she does not want to visit ever again.

It is not depressing, or not even sad.

But there are times, like when Celeste went with her family to Florida to avoid the winter blues, Norma is reminded that once upon a time her ancestors were multiple and no one would have expected that one of them would be left alone.

What makes certain families disappear while others continue to survive, to thrive and to multiply?

She thinks that the ones close to extinction have already exploited their reservoir of energy, the DNA that was allotted to them, while others are still dipping from the wells. And unless they use it all, they will still be thriving and multiplying.

"Love each other and multiply."

Perhaps her ancestry did not love each other enough or properly enough in order to go on and on, for the longest time.

A card arrives from Celeste with a view of the big hotel on the water and trees and flowers. Nice weather. It was pleasant to see: with signatures of Celeste, the husband and grown up children all having a wonderful time and sending their regards.

She is pleased. Her friends remembered her, remembered to write. When they come back, she and Celeste will have a good get-together. Perhaps they will have lunch in the neighboring restaurant or the trattoria.

Norma does not travel far any more. She did so, many times ago. But, perhaps, next year when Celeste travels to Florida, she may go with her. She would get a room close to theirs, walk into the sunny and fresh air and be pleased.

We will see.

Part II: Homes

Sleep

She has a dream. In the dream, early in the morning, she attends what seems to be a school or a seminar, with a group of friends. The teacher is kind: his voice is soft, at times whispering, loving. As if he is trying to wake up a sleeping beauty. She and her friends are in the house and she thinks that it is the teacher's house.

Then another group arrives and her friends are leaving one by one. She is left alone with people unknown to her. Is it another group that wishes to learn? They are all so friendly and are trying to engage her in conversation but she wants to leave. Her friends and colleagues are gone and she feels very alone. She is searching for her belongings and cannot find them.

In another room, the kind teacher has collected the newcomers and she listens in horror to his high-pitched, insulting voice as he is ordering the group into smaller rows and starts them marching.

A nightmare.

The house transforms itself into another, with dark panels and high ceilings. It sits on the top of the bare hill covered with dirt. It is full of witches and werewolves. She sees them and hears them. She walks through it frantically searching for an exit, meeting different people. Men and women ignore her, sneer at her and walk away. Then she meets others who cry and feel lost as she does. She tries to console them and tries to get out but cannot. The heavy, dark doors lead to nowhere. The place seated on the dark hill has no roads. She is searching for her belongings; her body is seminude and needs to be covered in order for her to somehow escape.

She wanders through the dark, big house with its large furniture, fuzzy in details as often it is in dreams. Finally, she finds a bed and falls into it trying to rest. In another bed, a young woman cries herself to sleep. Lying on the bed she starts to think that all this perhaps is not real. She feels a body next to her and realizes that her dog is trying to climb on her bed. She pushes him away and the effort wakes her up. She is back from the journey and in her old home. But is this her home? It is dark, narrow and depressing. The rooms are crowded with furniture, the walls covered with paintings and photographs. The Persian carpets on the floor look like old rags collecting dust. Dust has collected on the furniture, the television set and on the radio. The house has been left alone for too long.

How long has she been asleep? Wide-awake, she remembers her real home, the other place with high ceilings and whitewashed walls. And the big doors that lead to the balconies. She smells the salty air that is mixed with the odor of sail ropes and wet wood. Sleepy, somewhat hallucinatory, she walks though her real home as if reality did not exist. The reality is elsewhere, parked outside in the garages.

She looks for her jewelry and finds it missing. Did she bury it somewhere in a dark corner and now does not remember where it is? Did someone remove the precious gems in order to hide them from her or to store them in some unknown place?

The jewelry is missing. She already knows that she will not find it.

"Why is there always something to search for?" she is asking herself.

The summer is already here, and the heat is sweltering. She has a need to go into the water and to become a fish. When the weather becomes balmy, she drifts to the sacred island on the lagoon. The sanctuary. She will return to the house and perhaps continue her search. And find the exit from the bewitched, dark house.

Homeless

She lives in a house that is not hers. Could she hang her "hat" in it and call it her own? The sense of " transient" sticks with her and she wishes it would leave her. Permanently. Is there a bad energy in this place? She lights candles, burns sage branches and "hopes for eternity." "There should be some more stuff going on," she tells herself, "I am talking too much to myself. Perhaps I should find another house, another spot to call my own."

She imagines people coming and going, a table set with silver and china, bookshelves heavy, with books to be read in another hundred years. With ghosts walking in and out of the place: some good ones, some restless, some perhaps asking for forgiveness.

Her son's family: they are young and energetic, loving and enjoying life. The children are growing up with the promise of being bright and successful. Accomplishing a lot. And then leaving to meet their own destiny. Somewhere else?

In the morning, she reads the newspaper and becomes depressed.

It is depressing. It makes her feel helpless. Her aloneness hangs on her, over her body, over her head. Like a Damocles sword.

It is winter and the trees outdoors are covered with fresh snow. There is not a crystal-glistening of frost on them, no sparks, but still beautiful, pristine white, clean. She would like to reach out to the trees covered with snow. But the pathway is dangerous for her to walk on -- so her son thinks.

"Don't you dare to go out!" he tells her over the phone. "Do you have enough food in the house?" It is nice of him to call. To worry whether she will fall or get hungry.

"Do not worry about me," she answers, "I will be all right. Warm rooms, nice view, enough food."

He is satisfied and hangs up. His house is full of children, a spouse, her wife's relatives coming and going. People not afraid to fall and fracture a leg.

She is not afraid either. She calls friends, distant relatives and is chatting with them. That makes her loneliness less permanent.

"No reason to complain," she thinks. And yet... Why is she disliking the house that has large windows, where she can look outside to the trees and grassy slopes, that offers a vista to the distant city lights? In winter, she looks at the icicles covering the tree branches -- the frost-like broken pieces of precious crystal.

"It is breathtaking," her neighbor says. And it is.

To her, bad energy inhabits this lonesome house that she refuses to call home. Did she ever have a home of her own? Inhabiting diverse buildings at diverse times, she still remembers a large, chaotic old house that was destined to extinction. Not the house she was born in. It was the house she and her husband bought together when planning the family. A house in which other people previously lived and then got tired of it. Or could not afford it anymore. Or it became too large for them. Or without knowing it, they were on a pilgrimage, looking for other houses, changing houses until the end.

So now she lives alone in the house that is dainty, with a well-organized interior. There is no chaos in it, no coming or going of people, no large traffic of children and friends.

She thinks that she is not being fair to the house that offers her shelter, the commodities of modern living and a pleasant neighborhood.

"What is wrong with me?" she asks herself, walking through the house, burning candles and sage. "Is there a bad energy within?" Sometimes she thinks that being alone with her books in the warm rooms and high ceilings makes her a little crazy.

She does not wish her son to live in a place that would not be his own. How about an ancient old home on the corner of the narrow street, in the distant island with the view of the sea, with old wooden floors where pictures of great-grandfathers and grandmothers hang from the stone walls looking at him and at the generation to come. The old books that smell of eternity.

She feels better thinking about the old building, lights the candles and watches the bookshelves sagging under the weight of the books.

"It will take a hundred years to read all those books," she thinks again and tells herself: "Okay then, let's live to be a hundred." The last of sage finally burns out.

Shredding

Elaine sits in her small studio-room and shreds. She shreds old letters and notes that have piled up in boxes and old chests over the years of her life. They were transported faithfully over the years from one place to another in her many moves around the world.

The shredder makes noises and every once in a while, it stops working. The shredder is overheating. Elaine thinks that the shredder gets overwhelmed by the accumulation of the many fears, joys, sorrows and courage written onto these pages that she is now destroying. The cumulus of shreds can be put on the curb with other refuse to be collected in an orderly manner two times a week.

"I have lived for too long," she tells herself and continues with her work of destruction.

She thinks that after so many years, all becomes irrelevant. *Non sequitur.* It vanishes into the fog of half memory, not being there any more but only in the fog of passed times, passed days. It all becomes like a bad movie. What was considered perhaps great now appears long and boring and perhaps a little childish.

What is wrong with being childish?

She remembers the years passing by and it was always another day – tomorrow.

Always "mañana." And suddenly, there seems to be no mañana any more.

Running out of tomorrows does not disturb her. About what was considered important at the time, even heartbreaking, now appears as if a child is holding a broken toy in his or her lap. The mementos she is destroying are a testament of the long life (or so it seems to her) that she had fully lived. Sometimes pleasant or difficult and sometimes perhaps even irresponsible. Did God hold her hand in those irresponsible days?

A lost joy, lost friends, lost loves.

Elaine lives alone. Her children come to visit and take her for granted. Most of the time.

The waves of the ocean of life. Oceans change their colors, their structure, their temperature. How many undertows are there?

Dangerous undertows.

What may the present still bring? Past years were years of peace, of wellness. Were those selfish years? She does not know. She always "did her best." Perhaps the best was not adequate. The shredding continues. The shredding will become dust. Dust to dust.

There are many books in the place, on the shelves. Some reread over and over again, and some never opened or looked at. Like stillborn children, long forgotten, or the ones that were not loved and were overlooked and neglected.

It will take some time for Elaine to finish the shedding. Plastic bags are accumulating on the floor of the already crowded room. The books on the shelves will be left to Aurora, her daughter who likes old objects and old books. Aurora also likes old pictures of relatives long gone. Beautiful old pictures of great grandparents, of aunts and uncles, which hang in the family room and watch over them when they get together.

Those will go to Aurora. Will she leave them to her children or are we destined for extinction, our DNA not important or adequate anymore?

The world is full of hatred, intolerance and misconstrued beliefs. Elaine thinks that this, as everything else, shall also pass. "Tutto passa." Sometimes she would like to tell the ones who would listen that the destiny of all leaders, all "doges," is to perish. That revolutions kill their own as it did to

Robespierre, to Marat, to others and, after suppressing the tyranny, they may become tyrants themselves. But the world would not listen. The world never learns.

In her impossibility to be heard she continues in her small room to shred. The past. The irrelevant past.

"I have lived for so long," she thinks again. She does not wish to communicate with the world "out there." Once you get there, you start losing it slowly and systematically. And at the end, all repeats itself again.

She calls her daughter and she tells her:

"When winter comes, I would like to burn my shedding in your fireplace." No throwing it on the side of the road.

Aurora agrees:

"I love to use my fireplace. You are welcome to come and burn your stuff."

"There's a lot of it," Elaine says and Aurora responds:

"We'll do it in steps. Slowly. Over the period of the winter."

Then Aurora asks, "What did you shred?"

"Nothing important," Elaine answers, "some old papers that have no value any more."

Elaine thinks: "Hopefully, the world will calm down and there will be peace again. So that we can visit different parts of the world and share."

Share. Share wealth; share our different lives She talks to God and wishes for help.

The next day while visiting, Aurora looks at her mother. Aurora thinks:

"What was mother before? Before I was born? It would be interesting to know, perhaps I could write about it. If she would let me know. There is so much wisdom in mom. Where did she acquire all that?"

"I will give you the pictures of grandmother and grandfather," Elaine says, "Those are pictures of handsome people dressed in old-fashioned clothes. Pictures of good quality that do not fade away."

"Was this taken before the war?" Aurora asks.

"Before World War One," Elaine answers.

Aurora likes old pictures and old objects. She has an old coffee grinder that belonged to her great grandmother and still smells of coffee. And a few china pieces and little glasses for drinking grappa when having visitors. Grappa with dried figs. Nobody does this today. Scotch, vodka, bourbon.

Elaine thinks about the fireplace and thinks that she is getting old and sentimental. Overly sentimental. But only over grappa and figs, not the old letters that will be burning inside the stone fireplace in Aurora's old house.

"She is my child," Elaine thinks, "She likes solid, old houses with a stone fireplace in it."

Elaine can think dispassionately of her old friends wondering where are they today. Some have died. She knows that.

Jay, her husband was killed by a car while traversing the highway in a drunken stupor. She liked that man. She actually loved him. A drunkard, a liar, well-educated and angry at the world with baby blue eyes like her father's. Angry, abusive, at times loving. Dead husband crossing the highway in the middle of the night.

And Robert. Where is Robert now? Him with a vast renaissance knowledge but poor social graces.

"He could never wear a tuxedo," one of her friends has said of him.

The others? Not too many but her life has been long and full. So there were others. Not that it matters any more.

Elaine has cleaned the drawers and the old chests. Now she sits with her daughter in her daughter's house, thinks, and talks to Aurora.

The world around is full of hate, spilled blood, hunger and disease.

Where is humanity going? She thinks that the century will be like many others before. To wane into history, and no one will learn from it.

Aurora watches, her face still young, clean, serene. Aurora believes in goodness. In strength, in soul. Anger is not one of her qualities.

Anger is destructive, anger is a spoiler.

Perhaps Aurora will save the world? Elaine watches Aurora in the firelight. Might she, Elaine wonders and hopes – might all the Auroras- bring to this world a different kind of dawn?

Visit

June is driving alone toward the Jersey Shore in her big car that she does not like any more. It is an anachronism. She wants a small car that has four-wheel drive and is not a large consumer of gasoline. She wants something that she could and would drive in any kind of weather and whenever she would like to go. Not to worry if the doors get scratched or if someone hits it in a parking lot and then walks away without letting her know.

Calling for car repair, calling the insurance company, reporting the vandalism of the precious car that should stay in the garage in order not to be "hurt". Scratched, smashed, vandalized.

She drives to the shore and thinks this may be the last time. But probably not. How many last times did she perceive when the last time was not the last? It seems to her that she had been collecting "the last times" like someone collects gold coins, exotic flowers, and old perfume bottles. Or stamps.

She still has friends there. They have homes and jobs, businesses and boy friends. She travels there alone and thinks about it. She, too, once had a place there, but it did become too much for her. It was in an old building that reminded her of a medieval monastery, with thick walls, no elevator and steep stairs that were dangerous to climb. When she would reach the top, she could see the Atlantic, the sunrise in the early mornings. In the evenings, the sunsets with changing red colors and the sun disappearing slowly into another dimension. Brilliant, yellow, as if not wanting to go but unable to help itself.

In the past, it was so easy for her to walk up and down with groceries and books and bottles, but not anymore. So she gave it up, reluctantly, with sadness.

At present, she feels a stranger there, with no place of her own and this is the reason that whenever she goes there, for her it is supposedly "the last time".

("The last time I saw Paris". The movie. It comes to her).

She will meet her friend, Lynn. Lynn offers her hospitality but she herself does not feel comfortable. After so many years of togetherness and friendship, living next to each other in the different summers, she does not feel comfortable any more.

"We all have our lives to live," she thinks. Some are full of "doings." Some are small, every day "doings" and some not so small. Keeping the flame burning, doing special things or at least feeling that they are special.

With Lynn and others around her she could find herself feeling as though in a vacuum, the vacuum she had created by leaving, going in a different direction, abandoning the sun, the sand and the water and moving north. Did she have a choice? "There is always a possibility," she thinks "but a choice?"

Living in northern New Jersey, squished in by too many people, too many buildings, too many cars on the road. Feeling sorry for herself.

Being alone.

For years, being alone had been comfortable for her. Self sufficient, outgoing, enjoying her friends and their families. What happened? Did she change? Is life becoming old and boring?

At present she feels uncomfortable with her friends who live in large communities, having male friends with whom they share a bed, meals and the pleasure of togetherness. She has forgotten how all that feels and among them she feels strange. As if she had been inserted between their various activities with husbands, boyfriend's ex-husbands, ex-boyfriends and an occasional admirer.

But all this may be just her imagination.

"They are friends, my dear friends, part of my precious past, my memories and my growing in life. My past, everyday life."

Driving south, wondering whether any of them are waiting for her to go out for a walk, a dinner, a play.

A slight paranoia is creeping into her, tightening her chest. But is it paranoia or have they outgrow her so that present, she is only an incident, a pause between the happenings in which there may not, will not, be continuity?

Driving toward the shore and getting closer. The closer she gets, the more relaxed she is becoming. Is it the car with its rhythmic motion, or the expectation of seeing her friend that, in spite of everything, makes her calmer?

Driving on the Parkway, in the afternoon when there is no heavy traffic, with the green on both sides, on a summer day, it is actually pleasant. Yes, pleasant.

In fall, the trees change their colors and the road becomes surrounded with red. The red of the leaves.

The Parkway is not like the Turnpike, which is flat and bare with ugly commercial buildings that outsiders coming into New Jersey identify with New Jersey itself, and call the whole state ugly and unpleasant. They never see the rest of it. And though New Jersey is overcrowded and overbuilt, it is still a Garden State. Hopefully, for a long time. For how long a time?

When she arrives, she parks her car, picks up her bag and takes a walk. She inhales the fresh air and looks at the waves. She inhales deeply, her chest is expanding and if she did have a headache, it would be suddenly gone.

She feels rejuvenated: the vast space of the seashore.

Afterward, she walks toward her friend's home and they are there, some of them. Lynn, her friend of many years, is happy to see her, smiling, laughing, inviting her in. She walks in and all of a sudden she is relaxed, happy. Possibly, it will not be a last time.

They laugh. She thinks that because of laughter, they had remained good friends all these years. There is a comic side to every sad story.

Years back I had a place there. Peaceful, full of sunshine and sweet air. Now, I am just a guest although my friends assure me that I may stay as long as I wish.

I will stay only a few days. To stay longer makes me feel somehow sad. There should be no returning, no looking back. We try to avoid returning, but we are not always successful.

Before leaving for the shore I would be sitting at my present home, on the patio and getting a bit of sun. To replenish my body with vitamin D and thus avoid osteoporosis. I remember sitting on another patio and answering love letters to my faraway friend.

Too far away.

Or driving to the Jersey Shore. With R., whom I abandoned for someone else.

What was I thinking?

It is an early summer day, not oppressively hot or terribly humid. And I am driving to see my friend, Lynn, and to sit with her on her balcony, to look at the greens of the lawn and to talk.

Trying to help each other in answering questions that disturb us, that have disturbed us off and on through our lives.

Are there answers? Life is too intricate, the questions too complicated to answer and to solve the puzzles. Perhaps one should not try too hard, avoid tough questions, and live a simple life preparing oneself for the departure. But we do not do this, we simply cannot. It is not given to us. So we accept the challenges, accept the falls, the tragedies, the tragicomedies of life and the pleasures of success.

The pleasures of the spirit and the pleasures of the flesh.

Talking to each other, we might be able to solve some problems and or have a benefit to understand.

She meets Lynn and they talk, seated on the balcony that overlooks the greens. They talk of what has happened lately, or perhaps what has happened a long time ago.

The solving of life puzzles, sometime repeating what they already knew, possibly to find some point with a hidden meaning and to make clear something that had escaped them though time, through the years.

And they laugh through it all because, in every tragic story, there is a tragicomic streak.

Lynn is in a pensive mood. She wonders why most of her family has disappeared. Relatives who moved away and do not communicate any more. The others are close by in miles, but are still distant and not caring. Calling occasionally with ill-worded phrases, or to give the times of funerals or weddings. In past times, some of them would be looking for help, to be consoled in difficulties, "crying on her shoulders" and then disappearing into their own world with no further words or sharing. Or a thank you.

"Sometimes I feel like a cow that is giving milk when milk is needed," she laughs at the comparison but the humor is of the gallows sort.

"When I die, only my first and middle name will be on the grave. No last names. I do not have last names. They are gone with my mother, the stepfathers and the stepbrothers. And various aunts, cousins and pseudonephews. All these are pseudo, if I may add. Apparently, I do not belong. Innocence is ignorance, perhaps even stupidity. The stupidity of the milkable cow."

June laughs at the comparison. They both laugh at the tragicomedy of life.

Not long ago, Lynn did meet one of her cousins whom she had not seen in years. Not because she, Marisa, the cousin, lives somewhere distant in another part of the world, but because they had become estranged for some reason that Lynn does not remember. They had not seen each other for a long time. And then they met by accident at one of the book club meetings.

It was very casual, as if they were mere acquaintances smiling at each other pleasantly, not acknowledging each other as relatives, as friends. Lynn looked at her, listening to her converse with others. Telling them who she is. Telling them about her works, her trips, about her children from estranged husbands. So many different employments, different jobs and different skills, in many parts of the country. How many cities and towns did she inhabit and then leave? With no attachments, with no particular feelings about leaving. Starting something new with a certain serenity that bordered on indifference or apathy.

How does she feel?

How does she feel about Denver, about Boston, Florida, New Hampshire? Moving from one place to another, from one job, one profession to another?

Lynn listens to her and wonders. Her description of places makes Lynn feel as if she is seeing pictures taken by a poor quality camera, then discarded into a drawer and not looked at again. With her monotonous voice, pleasant, articulate, she describes her work, the places she lived in, and the reasons for abandoning them to move somewhere else. All orderly and with no upsets.

Lynn listens to her, watching her face without trying to interrupt. Or to ask questions, to acknowledge her, her blood relative whom she did not see in a long time, about whom she recognizes only the face.

Was Marissa always like that? Times ago they were relatives, they were friends. And now, there is nothing. At the end they just said good-bye, pleasantly, the cousin smiling and Lynn serious and a bit stand-offish.

Was she always like this?

Marissa lives close now back, in the old homestead. It is easy to keep one's distance in their over populated towns and cities where one does not have to meet unless one wants to. Lynn does not particularly care to meet Marissa again. They are relatives and had been friends some distant time ago. And now there is nothing. Some colors, some descriptions, some stories as if they happened to someone else. Lynn cannot help from wondering how someone could be moving though life like that. A bit here, a bit there, changing lifestyles, changing passages and callings, taking all that with no hurt, no regrets.

Do they have the same or similar genes? Or are there mutations ending the tribe, ending the genealogy?

She remembers Marissa as vivacious, pleasant, funny. She still may be all that. Lynn is not going to find out.

It is like a story happening to someone else.

Lynn tells all this to June and she listens and understands Lynn's amazement at such behavior. But there is nothing she can add to the story to make it more logical, more acceptable.

"Just take it as someone else's reality," she tells her, "and do not try to understand or solve the how and why of it."

"Is this disturbing you?" She asks Lynn.

Lynn answers, "Possibly – but only because Marissa and I are relatives. Is there a streak of this in me also?"

"I do not think so," Lynn adds quickly.

And two of them continue enjoying the gentle ocean breeze in the afternoon that is slowly becoming evening.

Sitting on the balcony June wonders about Lynn. Why Lynn has nothing to say about her mother? Why is she talking about a cousin whom she did not see for so long?

It is difficult to talk about matters that still hurt. It is better to forget. It would still be better to forget and only to remember the good. How much of the good was there?

The summer at the beach.

The fishing boats, all different sizes, on the water surface. A good number of them. June never did any fishing. She never had a boat no matter how big or small it could have been. She used to swim in the ocean but now it was too dangerous. For her, at present, the ocean is too powerful. It calms down somewhat in the evening hours. Still, it is not the Mediterranean. Or the Adriatic. But the air and the breeze make it worth sitting on the veranda in Lynn's home on the Shore.

A Day in the Life of Maggy Brown

A house is like a lover. Once you have it, you start to find all the missing parts, all the inadequacies you did not notice before.

"Love at first sight."

You walk through the rooms and the rooms are too large or too small. The floors are nude and the noises you make walking remind you that you are alone and the only friend you have is the echo your steps make on the bare, wooden floor. The desk on which you write is crowded with papers and books.

Do you want to read all those books? They will bore you and they may make you cry because there is nothing in them that could make your heart beat faster. It has all been said before and no one is listening.

Friends are gone. Only robots remain and you wish to see a real face. A human face.

Do you really love humans? Or did they also disappear into nothingness, and you cannot find them any more? Just a peek: a hand to grab, a morning hello.

The rain is beating on the dormers, the symphony of it, repetitious and monotonous.

Waiting for the phone to ring. Waiting for the name of the caller to appear on the screen and then hang up since it is someone wishing to sell you something. Is this better than the silence?

You collect your pocketbook, a bag with dry cleaning, your soiled tablecloth and you go to run your chores. You wish to have a conversation with someone: The dry cleaning lady. The store clerk.

The dry cleaning lady smiles pleasantly and accepts your bag with a tablecloth, then writes a ticket for you. "Have a nice day."

The store clerk looks at you and gives you the merchandise. You try to smile and to say something. Perhaps, "What a humid, rainy day," but you say nothing and he does not smile. You leave with your acquisitions; the side streets are almost empty when you drive home.

The house is like a lover: inviting in the beginning, and then showing all its defects, all its shortcomings.

"Is there anything for me to do?"

Your "alter ego," your "doppelganger" comes out of the woodwork and talks to you, telling you that you are all wrong. "You can call a friend and go out for lunch. Did you forget that the furnace needs repair and the man is coming tomorrow? It is so spacious here and you can sit and read the latest book you have picked up at the library."

Why read? Why become angry at the sad face the world is presenting to you and about which you cannot do anything?

Yesterday is gone.

Today is gray, boring and does not give any pleasure.

Tomorrow.

The rain is beating the dormers and then stops altogether. The patio is glistening. Washed out, its floor is made of a red wood of undetermined provenance. You have no knowledge about the trees, the quality of wood on the patio, of the roof that is solid and not leaking.

Get me out of here.

"I want to be taken out for a ride. Or on the train to the Promised Land. I want my heart to start beating fast. I am looking for old friends to say hello to, and to laugh at the world and heaven and to the geysers that spurt hot water at the desert.

(Does this exist?)

I would like to be laughing. Laughing incessantly like a happy clown. Are there happy clowns in the world? Have there ever been happy clowns?"

The "alter ego" talks again: "There is so much you can do. Many positive doings. Many every day positive deeds, positive pleasures, like a cup of hot tea or coffee with brown sugar and perhaps a cookie."

Would you like a cookie? Or a slice of panetone?

Is it raining in the Andes? Or is a drought taking over their continents where people are suffering of malnutrition or dying of malaria?

The "alter ego" says: "This is not your problem. Not your problem at all. Get your act together."

She is waiting for sun. For a sunshine. She wants to sit out on the patio, get sunburned, be covered with the leaves that are falling from the tall trees.

Is it too much to ask?

The house is silent once more, the floors are still bare and the echo of her steps are reminding her that the house is like a lover. It seems so perfect, so inviting. And then, it comes again -- one discovers the missing parts, the need for repairs.

She tries to listen to the heartbeat, to the Universe, but the Universe does not talk. The Universe is deaf. It does not communicate with her. It is looking the other way.

Part III: Other Stories

After the Fall

What do I remember about that fateful morning when I collapsed on the floor of the bathroom, after washing the sleep out of my eyes?

Early morning, the sun just peeking out on the east over the ocean. Bloody beautiful. Sun like blood. And my blood collecting into an ugly embolus-clot and reaching my brain.

My husband found me on the floor after wondering why I was taking so long to get to the breakfast table. Darkness. I presume that I was twitching, salivating. Possibly vomiting. Vomiting bile, gooey, amorphous and ugly blobs of vomitus.

I, this beautiful, sophisticated and elegant woman, covered with saliva and vomit on the bathroom floor.

I was a person who practiced yoga and reiki, played the violin, lived outdoors and on one occasion climbed part of Mount Everest. And, on the morning of a day that was promising to be great, it all came crashing in on me in the form of a gooey little glob of thickened blood, my own blood, reaching my brain.

My own blood.

Why did my body betray me, me who has cherished it, washed it in lavender and anointed it with precious oils in order to keep it safe? My body -- a beautiful container of my achievements?

At present, I am paralyzed. My left arm is hanging lifeless by my side, and my left leg is encased in metal and wires.

In the hospital, after days of agony and uncertainty, my brain did resurrect and started working again. That same brain that received the blood clot causing all the damage is again functioning.

Was this a miracle?

Or was this the revenge of some unknown deity that became jealous of who I was?

At present, I limp around the house unable to walk the steps to my second floor, a place where I have collected the pieces and mementos of my interesting life. In the beginning of this journey and lying in the hospital beds, I tried to recuperate as much as possible of my old self. Some of it came back, and some did not.

My face is the same face that I had before, slightly thinner, somewhat haggard but (I think) still the same face that my husband loved and my children cherished. My husband -- who loved my vitality and would be amused by all the different ways I experienced life and all the different ways I lived through it. We complemented each other, he so stable in his ways, a rock to which I always returned, eager, sometimes tired and exhausted by my excursion into life. Finding him always there with a big smile, amused and pleased to have me back with him.

The understanding.

And the changing of things.

Am I still the same person? I am going through physical therapy and I am trying to walk again. Trying to drive a special kind of car adjusted to my malfunction.

Will our lives together be different?

The friends that I had are disappearing slowly; some possibly unable to see me in the way I am now. I would like to shout, to tell them loudly:

"It is still me, the same person, the same mind. Only the body is different. Still trying to live, to walk, and to drive a car, to perhaps read a book. Do not be afraid. Do not be horrified."

I do not say these things and we try to communicate with each other by keeping up small talk. But I see their faces contorted and their eyes turning repeatedly toward my arm and my leg that are not functioning as they should be. So little by little my friends disappear, occasionally calling, occasionally sending a small note on a small card.

I understand.

They are used to seeing me differently, to experiencing me differently and perhaps living somewhat vicariously through my way of life.

I live with my husband in a different house now. We have abandoned the house to which I would always return -- where my husband and I shared our days and raised our children. Now I live in a house that is flat and accessible to accommodate my disability but also pleasant, having moved into it the objects that we have accumulated in our lives together.

I listen to music more now than before. Sometimes I think that the Universe wanted me to stop and to nurture a part of me that is more contemplative, more intuitive and "introverted".

Why use such drastic way to bring me to it?

When I was in the hospital and concentrating on my physicality, I missed many kind notes and letters from my friend Jean. Then, at home, where I was putting my crippled life together, it so happened that in a basket with my knitting I found her messages, all at once. So many messages she sent to me that I never received while in my hospital rooms.

I remember her fondly, as being proper, somewhat conventional, but always open to learning new things. Together, we tried to learn numerology, reiki and playing golf, for we liked the outdoors.

Golf was such a wonderful game to play. Walking through the fields, enjoying open spaces. Using one's physicality to chase the little ball in different directions. And Jean, like a neophyte, following and trying to learn.

Her notes and letters brought to me the memories of all this. Us, walking through the grass, after the ball, having the sun in our faces and trying to protect ourselves from its rays.

Not feeling sorry for myself, I called her and inquired about our mutual friend Paula with whom I used to play regularly.

"Call her," I said, "get together with her and play. And when you are playing, you both think of me."

It was not sentimentality. It was my participation with them as if I were there. And she promised that she would do it.

I know that Jean is horrified by the way I look now. She is an aesthete, not able to imagine anyone having a brace on their leg, shuffling that same leg along, and the arm hanging lifeless on the side of their body.

She would consider something like that "miserable". A person like that to be pitied and to keep herself locked in a dark room not to be seen by healthy people, beautiful people.

But I like her, because she is not "nasty." She would not sneer at the likes of me, or with malice tell her acquaintances:

"Poor Ely, look at her. And she was so alive and beautiful."

Rather, she will say:

"I know, poor Ely." But it would be a genuine feeling of sorrow because I could not be considered beautiful any more.

Listening to music, shuffling through the new habitat that has no steps to climb, I think of her and the friend with whom she will meet to play golf.

They will talk about me. And be sorry because I cannot be there with them.

"But think of me," I have said. "And if you think of me, part of me will be there."

How at peace am I with myself? I notice now things that before I would perhaps just pass by or take for granted. In my other busy life, I would rush past the sunsets and sunrises thinking that they were "nice", "beautiful", "lovely." Now, I look at it with different eyes, have a different perception.

I observe the sea shimmering in the sun, the vastness of it, the little sailboats looking like many little toys scattered on the surface, with toy people sitting in them and smelling the salt. Perhaps with no other feeling or thoughts in their toy heads but the sensation of smell, of sight, or the feeling of the slight breeze.

Simple sensations.

No need for expensive perfumes, nail lacquer, rouged lips.

Is it so? Or am I just experiencing this at present, since I cannot pick up my own toys and fly with them around the world.

I do not care. All this is beautiful.

I may write this to my friend Jean but I do not think that she would understand. She will tell Paula, our other friend while playing golf with her:

"Poor Ely. She is trying hard to be brave."

Summer arrives, not yet hot, not yet oppressively humid, forcing us to stay indoors in our artificious houses over-chilled by central air. The air is clear and warm today, with the sun peeking through sparse patches of clouds, timidly making us aware of its presence.

In this early summer sun, there is a sense of the passing of time, a loneliness that cannot be filled, an emptiness of feelings. In the distance, the laughing and crying of children on the seashore, the sweating of bodies, the smell of burnt barbeque meat. The memories, the coming back of long-past happenings. And the melancholy of silence in the afternoon siesta.

"Pick up the book, Ely, and sit on the balcony and think that, in spite of everything, you may consider yourself lucky."

But I do not feel very lucky. I have this little wish to go to the golf course, sit in the golf cart and be driven around from one hole to another, pretending that I am there to play. I ask only for the green of the fresh grass on a conventional golf course. Just a spread of grass with gentle slopes and small flags placed in the spots where they should be. No altipiani, no Cordilleras.

My balcony is made of a silence, with distant sounds of passed times and rememberings, remembrances and a rumbling of the hi-tech of the cities.

What am I waiting for?

I want to move, to drag my dead limbs outdoors, to participate.

What am I doing on this balcony, alone; while the world is living in the summer heat?

My husband and my children consider me unreasonable. They want me protected from myself in a flat house on the seashore.

Michael collects his maps and his business tools, ready to leave the house. He looks at me and says:

"See you in a while. You will be all right?"

I nod my head, look at him and smile: "Yes, I am all right," and I add, "When are you returning?" then quickly:"We'll have supper together."

He does not think that I am capable anymore to prepare a supper.

"Trust me," I say, "I will prepare something simple."

He looks at me and smiles. Is he trying to get away quickly or is this only my imagination? He leaves, promising to be back soon.

I think: "It would have been so wonderful to spend free time together. If I were healthy and all in one piece. All pieces intact."

Then I dream of the Cordillera Blanca and sit back in my chair.

Why the Cordillera? I was never there. Was I there perhaps in a past life? One of my past lives? Did I meet my end up there in a mountain disaster only to return to this civilized country where death comes in slow motion and tries to sneak in past the contraptions created by high technology?

Who knows? Would it be better, perhaps, to perish in the Cordillera?

How do you die in the Cordillera? What kind of accident would have to happen?

I do not know.

I do not know anything about these high mountains, but I imagine open spaces and a lot of clean air. Nothing else. I t is ignorance or arrogance of me to think about these mountains? At present, I want to get onto the golf cart and move across the golf course watching, observing, and thinking what I would do there if I were not crippled.

But I am still I, Ely.

"Cogito ergo sum".

Only the golf cart. No Cordillera, for now.

Michael spends less and less time in our house on the water. He finds excuses to leave as often as he can. For work, for pleasure, for seeing his old buddies. Somehow, to lead a life that is comfortable and without me in it.

Is this true?

Or am I being a cripple who is becoming more and more intolerant and at the same time more demanding?

I do not think so.

We are going to move again. They want me close to my grown up children, who have their own families, and close to the hospitals in case I develop some other inconvenient health problem. A woman is coming in to help pack our belongings.

The house they found is also flat; it is comfortable, full of light but somewhat far from the ocean. No more toy boats and toy people to observe.

Michael is pleasant. Michael is caring. He also walks away whenever he can, drives away in his car, does his "thing".

Michael, I need you.

Michael, come back to me. I write a letter to my friend Jean and wish that she would come and visit with me. And talk to me. At present, she is taking care of an old aunt. Her children live close but have their own agenda. The aunt is an old crotchety lady with innumerable complaints and a poor disposition. Doesn't the old aunt realize that eventually we are all left alone?

Jean has a compulsion to help, always to help. I wish that she would come, to talk to me, not to help me.

I help myself. I want to help myself.

This is the third house I will be moving into in a short time. The first was my home and the others are just habitats. The poet's words come to me often, the poem I thought I had long forgotten. "Partir c'est mourir un peu."

"Michael, be here with me in the new strange house close to the hospitals."

"Jean, come and visit so that we can talk and perhaps take a walk, however difficult the walk may be on the green slopes."

Ely called:

"Jean, please come visit with me."

Jean looks at herself in the mirror: there are bags forming under her eyes, and there are fine lines around her mouth. She does not go into the sun any more, and uses creams that are supposedly rejuvenating, promise a smooth skin and the disappearance of wrinkles. How she would like to go into the sun and get a healthy tan. Instead, she sits in her comfortable home where she lives with an aunt who is old and demanding, and constantly complaining of her arthritic back.

"Try not to dwell on it," Jean tells her. "Try to watch television or read a magazine. If you do this, the pain may be less pronounced, more tolerable." But the old lady pays no attention. She loves to complain. She loves her painful back.

Jean thinks:

Whatever happened to all the past times? Marriage. The children growing. Her husband. A lady friend said to her years back: "So this is the way of men. If they cannot leave us any other way, then they die on us."

It was told to her a long time ago, but every so often it comes back to her. Her husband had died on her. Left her. Suddenly.

Her children speak to her. Occasionally. From a distance. They are restless, moving from place to place, searching for betterment. A different generation. She takes it all with tolerance. Her Latin comes to her: "O tempora, o mores." Sometimes it is lonesome. And sometime it is boring.

She thinks of Ely. Ely has always been so vital, so adventurous. In spite of her disability, Ely is still strong with perhaps a touch of anxiety in her last message.

Jean looks into the mirror again, seeing herself as she appears now.

She thinks: "In spite of wrinkles I am still beautiful."

She will put her old aunt into the convalescent home for a few weeks, get into her car and drive to Ely. They will talk, remember and drive a golf cart though the fresh grass on the golf course.

Remembering Laura

It was on the Christmas Eve that you did decide to leave us.

You never wanted to be sick, never wanted anyone to know or suspect that you could be sick.

Such mystery, such secretiveness.

I remember your kindness the time I had a broken ankle. You took me around in your car and we went through the park to see the cherry blossoms. The whole park full of trees with magnificent blossoms, white, yellow, pink. You were kind that day and I was grateful. Cherry blossoms last a very short time, one, mostly two weeks in May, and then the park returns back to being just a regular, everyday park. Nothing to specifically look for. You drove. I watched. Pleasant, relaxing times.

Sometimes you could make me angry about your fancy ways and old world style but that was you. Occasionally I would let you know that the world had changed for the better and sometimes for the worse, but you were who you were: a proper, well behaved girl from a good family, carrying a certain amount of narrowness of mind -- what I considered frivolous and superficial.

I at times suspected that underneath all that another persona was hiding, occasionally surfacing, a slightly calculating persona carrying some unpleasant or troublesome secret from a long, abandoned past. Perhaps this was only my imagination. Now, I will never know. Because you are gone.

Laura

A small, peaceful town seemed to serve as a solution to her solitary existence. It was to be a last stop. A last stop on an imaginary railroad station that she had never used before. A little fantasy about quiet and undisturbing days. Her problem was that she was not born to be undisturbing. Sitting in the new house she found herself to be short of breath and, being deprived of her natural restlessness, gave her a sickly feeling. She started driving around the neighborhood, slowly, attentive to road signs, attentive to other cars. Her car a hiding place.

Am I slowing down, my reflexes failing, and my brain shrinking, diminishing, malfunctioning? The double standard that I have built for myself: a need for peacefulness and retreat and at the same time experiencing a shortness of breath and a sensation that I am disintegrating into non-action.

Having a few friends only that were still alive.

Megan comes to visit me and we sit on the veranda, in autumn, amid leaves that are falling from tall trees and talk about times passed. Actually, only about recent past times. The last ten years or so. The rest of my life to my friends is a "Tabula rasa" There is almost nothing there or this is how I perceive it. Megan and I eat cookies and have a glass of Perrier. We laugh, sometimes remembering some of our trips and the happenings that we could laugh about. I feel fine then as if resurrected and as if I never had moved away from the place in which I have spent most of my days.

She is one of the last friends left, somewhat younger than I and healthier (I think). We see each other and when we do not, we call each other and speak on the phone. She can be difficult sometimes: opinionated, passionate about problems and themes that to me are totally indifferent. Sometimes she accuses me of being petty. We come from different backgrounds. But we are friends. She calls me and I tell her:

"Thank you for being my friend."

She does not understand why I repeat that often. To her, it is spontaneous to be my friend.

I remember my childhood: my loving parents, my very young days. Then after that I do not remember. I do not talk about myself to others. But I like to have friends and I need them.

"Thank you for being my friend."

I have moved away since my ailments are getting more pronounced and more visible to people around me. When I walk, I am uneasy and I limp slightly. My back (or is it my hip?) is being painful. It is painful for me to walk and embarrassing to limp.

When we go out I walk arm in arm with her and we walk slowly as if we were in a deep description of something very important. Not to make the rest of the world see that I am, well, becoming crippled. No, that is too strong a word. Just slightly "indisposed."

"Thank you for being my friend."

I am driving on the main artery where my new home is. I am going home. Behind me a string of cars are following. They are getting closer and closer to me, and starting to toot their horns "beebeep" "beebeep".

"Don't you see that I am looking for a driveway?" I scream in my car, upset, angry, continuing the search to the entrance of the driveway. Of course no one hears. No one cares that I am living on this street and that my driveway is hidden and narrow. This is my home.

"Please leave me alone, please let me get into my house."

I feel as if I am invisible. Am I ugly? Am I an alien precipitated from another planet into this quaint pseudosophisticated environment?

Could this all be my imagination?

The town is only a short distance from where I have lived all these years and now it seems that I am in a hostile, angry world that is not my own.

My hip (or is it my back?) is hurting me, but I do not tell acquaintances or Megan that it is really serious. I do not want to be sick. I do not want to be old. I continue to attend luncheons and the meetings of charitable organizations. There are less and less people I know. Some have moved away, some have died.

I go to see a doctor but it is almost like a social visit. I do not tell him much about my pain and where exactly is located. I ask for some pain medication, assuring him that it is only a passing discomfort.

It is not as if I wanted to die. I actually wanted to live -- but to live on my own terms.

Years ago, I was diagnosed with cancer. Nobody knew that except Megan. I had some surgery. Then I forgot about it. Megan would ask occasionally but I would always cut it short, assuring her that I was doing well. No one in my family had ever had cancer. I had always been healthy. My blood pressure, my eyesight, all was good. Why would anyone even imagine that I might be ill?

I am driving through my new neighborhood where I am not known, and no one approaches me.

Today, I have smashed my car into the garage door, taking a narrow sweep at the entrance and scraping the whole left side. Tomorrow I will take the car to be repaired. No one will know. Not even Megan.

Please be my friend.

Thank you for being my friend.

I am almost glad that the place I had moved into is not to my liking and that I do not feel comfortable and adjusted to the house itself.

I wish to take a bath. I used to sit in my tub for hours but now the tub seems too steep, the water too hot or too cold, hard water full of calcium salts.

What a way to go.

I have squirrels and chipmunks in my backyard and I saw a deer traversing the road when driving in my car. Loving animals had always been my joy. Where are the humans?

I miss not going into New York. I would love to see the exhibit of "El Greco to Picasso" at the Guggenheim. I would love to see El Greco again. He was one of my favorites. I had always liked the elongated, ascetic faces and long, thin bodies of people he painted. But I do not drive into New York anymore. It has been for some time now. How sad.

Megan has called to find out how I am feeling and how the new house is coming along.

"I am good," I say. "I am getting used to the house. I have put more paintings on the wall. All by myself," I add.

You should not do that," Megan says. "It is too heavy for you. Will you ask someone to help?" Then Megan says: "We're having an incredible balmy winter. Let's go out to lunch."

"Let's go," I answer. "Give me time to get ready."

She will pick me up and we will go to lunch.

We used to go into New York, alone or with a group, and it seemed so easy then. Different groups, mostly museum members. With a bus. Or sometimes we would go and Megan would drive. I do not want to ask Megan if she drives into New York anymore. Probably not. Heavy traffic. Waiting at the entrance to the tunnel for too long. Crowds.

I miss New York. I want to go to New York again, perhaps one more time. The city I love. You were a part of my life and you still are.

Occasionally, like a big tidal wave, memories come to me and I can see all the sunshine that I always loved and the young days of running up the beach and the boys that had courted me. And then again the curtain falls and I am alone with myself, realizing that my head hurts and I cannot hear the voices that seem to be around the room, perhaps across a table. Which table? So much pretending. I cannot do it anymore.

I have had a good life to the last.

Till now.

How sad. Is there a trace of us left somewhere?

The day is getting gray. Or is it my room that is getting dark and gray?

Thank you for being my friend.

And then she died.

A Woman

A woman wrapped in a large, black cloak sits in the corner of a busy street, a short distance from a ferryboat landing. People around her move swiftly back and forth trying to leave the area. Some buy cheap souvenirs from vendors: t-shirts, masks, postcards.

People, people, people.

Not offensive, not crude, just a nondescript multitude of different mixtures of nationalities and ethnicities. In a corner, the woman is sitting on the ground with a hand outstretched and a small metal container in hand, begging for money. She is completely covered with a black cloth and she does not move. Her hand, with a plate, sticks out of the black garment -- just the hand. There is a large, white cloth covering her head and her face, making you wonder how she is able to breathe.

Perhaps she is not real. Perchance she is a ghost, seated on the ancient stones of the long-gone Venetian Empire.

Marbella also passes her by, with her group of friends who are anxious to see the Basilica. "The Basilica of Gold" in the heart of Venice. Covered with mosaics and marble, it shines in the Venetian sun like an enormous, expensive jewel. It is a mixture of styles, having been alive through many centuries and still unique in its beauty and its perfection.

Marbella wants to see the horses. There are four horses in the Basilica's indoor museum. Centuries back, when Venice sacked Constantinople during the Crusades, the horses were transported from the crumbling Byzantium to the mighty Serenissima. Now they are hidden in the dark interior of the museum, put there to save them from the bad weather and the industrial soot. *Sic transit gloria mundi.*

Their replicas are outside on the loggia for all to see, but the "green ones" are protected. When Marbella sees them, they are in motion, their nostrils flaring and bodies streaked with gold. Are they sweating gold in the penumbra of the place?

Marbella had climbed steep stone steps to get to them, and afterward, descending the treacherous steps and exiting outdoors, she remembered the woman sitting on the street corner. Who brought her here, silent and invisible, to collect coins from the tourists' throngs, on the bank of the Grand Canal? Perhaps she is a remnant of the carnival season where reality remains hidden under the masquerade. Except that the Carnevale is long gone, and the little metal container protruding under the dark cloth tells unequivocally that there is a beggar waiting for a donation.

Marbella comes closer and puts a few coins into the outstretched hand with the metal box. She bends and tries to see her face and asks her first in Italian, and then in English:

"How are you lady? Are you all right?"

Between the folds of the white shroud, two dark eyes look towards her with no interest and no expression. She says in a monotone:

"Thank you," And repeats again. "Thank you, thank you."

"May I see your face?" Marbella asks again, unable to go her own way. The dark eyes look at her as if not seeing. There are no signs of marvel, of annoyance or pleasure.

The woman repeats again robotically the same phrase:

"Thank you, thank you."

Marbella does not insist. She feels a sense of detachment, almost hostility. As if the thank you actually means, "Go away." And she goes away.

Back home in the United States, she thinks of the woman often and experiences a sense of helplessness. She feels that the dark eyes looking at her could have been blue, green or hazel, representing many women from distant and diverse countries, forced into begging or something worse.

In her warm and comfortable home, Marbella remembers the faceless woman that she left on the corner close to the ferryboat station. Could she have done something? Not much. Just a few coins into the extended hand. But – couldn't she have done something?

It Could Be Worse

Why are we always complaining so much, always finding fault with everything and everyone? Do we have too much time on our hands and not enough sorrow, not enough troubles to take away our complacency?

In the Tuareg country, there is a drought and the lack of rain has destroyed the crops. The animals are dying because of lack of food and lack of water. And humans are dying too.

We walk down the street with rain beating on us, wetting our hair, destroying our shoes and our dresses. When we finally arrive and enter into our warm homes, we take off our wet garments, take a hot shower and put some dry clothes on.

Meanwhile, in Niger, a young mother suffers the pain of childbirth and there is no one to help her. After a long time, days perhaps, the child is stillborn and the mother also may be dead. A young mother, a very young mother that should not be dying. Should not be dead. But she is.

And we are not. We are doing well. Of course, there may be difficulties, even depravations. Are we depraved? Do we ever think? Do we sometimes think in our warm homes, sipping our coffee and taking our hot showers about the young mother in Niger dying in childbirth?

Do we think?

What do we do? Are we so bad? Is it all so bad? We think and do, and hope and dream, and yet when someone tells us, we are horrified. So what do we do?

What would you do?

A Cat in the Corner

A cat sits on her special spot in the corner of the living room. She watches intensely what Grace is doing. Grace sitting on the couch, watching television and having a drink.

Cat likes Grace. Grace was the one who saved her from the shelter where she was slowly losing her mind. With her cat's mind she was able to observe the people around. And other cats and other animals locked in cages. The cages smelled. The animals in them had also a foul odor of neglect. They were suffering from malnutrition and the lack of love.

Now, with Grace, her fur is white again and between her eyebrows her green eyes observe Grace carefully, wondering why Grace has a glass in her hand. Grace has a glass in her hand all too often.

Cat wonders why.

Sitting in the corner, the Cat thinks of moving closer, to put her head in Grace's lap and perhaps to take a nap. The two of them may take a nap together.

Cat starts to purr, and thinks that her purring may bring her to Grace's attention. It may make Grace put the glass on the table and just sit back on the comfortable couch in order that Cat may put her head in Grace's lap and they may take a nap together.

But Grace pays her no attention and continues her drinking from the glass. Her eyes are distant as if observing some faraway horizons.

What has a cat to do, but sit and purr softly as if a lullaby is offered to the sitting friend, who is not paying attention to the cat's purring and to any object around her?

The television is on, but most probably Grace is nor watching. Sipping from her glass, she is oblivious to her surrounding, ignoring her cat, ignoring the television. And ignoring the world that moves outside in its own perpetual "danse macabre."

Cat purrs and waits.

Cat thinks that she, in this moment, is the only living connection for Grace with the world that Grace is ignoring and perhaps despising. She just is abandoning herself to the fumes and the evaporations that are concentrated in the glass from which she drinks.

The rituals that are repeated every day. And with every day are lasting longer and longer.

Does the purring of the cat keep Grace breathing? If there will be no more purring will the breathing stop? And will the empty glass fall to the floor and break itself into many little smithereens?

Cat continues to purr and then slowly and tentatively changes the position. She moves slowly in Grace's lap.

Grace sits still, with the glass in her hand and with her eyes closed. She looks peaceful.

Is she still breathing?

After The Fall II

The tall trees around her home partially isolating her from the neighbors who were into their own small world, whatever that could have been. Not a pleasant neighborhood. "Ognuno per se stesso e Dio per tutti," her grandmother would say and she had a great common sense.

Her grown children lived in the next town that was more cosmopolitanized and visited her regularly. Perhaps not often enough. Or so she thought. Phone calls every two or three days and then visits. Nice visits, helping repair the broken utensils or taking old books and newspapers to the recycling bin.

Not bad.

She used to sit in the garden on the patio and read. Or sun for short periods between reading books or journals in order to supply herself with enough vitamin D. She also drove into the town where she used to live, where there were galleries, a museum and quite a few good restaurants.

She enjoyed the activities she had.

The trees in the garden, the sunning on the patio. The sunsets with her sitting outdoors and then, when the twilight would become too pronounced, getting into the house.

And then she fell. She fell down the two steps leading from the kitchen into the dining room. The steps were wide and flat and never considered a danger. The rest of the house was flat, a ranch house. No other steps.

Trying to get up, checking her shoulders and wrists and finding them all intact, she tried to stand up but could not. Her right leg was lying sideways in a strange position, away from her body. Her body was shaking, and her eyesight was blurred. After the shaking subsided, pain started intense and unbearable, coming from her right hip. Lying on the floor of the dining room, she lost consciousness.

The rain was beating on the dormers above and the wind was shaking the trees around the house. The noise of it must have woken her up. She did not know why she was lying on the floor of the dining room with her right leg twisted and distant like an alien object, not belonging to her body at all.

The pain. The pain was real and coming from the direction of the right leg.

"Do not move. Think of what had happened. Was in the afternoon and you were running to the door to collect the mail? Or was it simply someone ringing the door bell and then leaving since no one was answering the bell? Was it something else?"

It took some time to remember. She simply tripped. Tripped and fell.

It seemed that something like this could happen. The fragility of bones, the consequence of aging. She never expected that it might happen to her. Being proud of her body, her apparent strength, the lack of serious illnesses. Her body shook again. She fell asleep or perhaps, she fainted again.

The pain woke her up and she wondered what would happen to her if her son did not show up at her home after not being able to reach her by phone. Perhaps she would die in the meantime from hunger, dehydration or perhaps just from pain. How much physical pain can the human body tolerate? Do people that were tortured and have survived ever explained how much it would take to be killed by mere physical pain and would it, in this condition, become a welcomed end?

The thoughts coming and going, floating through the day (or was it night?) like birds in flight, while she lay on the floor, her distorted leg distant as if not her own anymore but an alien body, an enemy that is torturing her slowly, off and on as if playing some cruel games with her. And when it was too painful to tolerate, it would let her faint and drift into unconsciousness.

She wondered if death would come before she could be saved and what she would have missed the most from her life, past and present.

Living in the house that was temporary but still her own, still being her own person and, to a point, her own master. A small sleepy town, a bedroom town as a friend once called it. She was a stranger to the town itself, surrounded by tall maple trees. Some of them too old to last much longer. And the tall grassy plants with white little flowers growing haphazardly, giving her the feeling of being outside the town, its sleepy inhabitants with their banal routines. Honest inhabitants of their small fiefdom.

She would miss the trees around the house, and the little white wild flowers, even the leaves that abundantly would cover the outside of the house. The steps, the driveway, the lawn. The golden carpet of the fallen leaves. The autumn time.

She heard the noise of the radiators and knows that the summer is over. It is late in the fall and the heat is on. The trees will be bare soon. The grass is dying but it will resurrect again in spring. What has happened to the little animals that frequently scurry through the tall grass? The birds. She is sorry for not putting any birdseed in the bird feeder. She wanted to do it so many times, but somehow never did. And it is too late now. It is because of the autumn and because of her leg.

She tries to think how happy or unhappy she was in her younger days. She was away from home once. Was it at school or was it in summer season? Being away from home somewhere. Was this in another world, in another life? Was mother a good person? Did mother care? It took her a long time to come and retrieve her from the house, in the valley, surrounded by small trees and vegetable patches.

"What kind of fantasy was that? " she thinks and she is back among the maple trees, the grass and the unpaved driveway as she is coming back from running away, once long ago. No mother to come to pick her up now, if even sometime late.

Did mother wait too long, perhaps, hoping to get rid of her? Finally she did pick her up and brought her home. Boring home. It was such a long time ago and perhaps it was not true at all. The loneliness. The boredom of the young years.

Her son is to call, to find out how is she doing. He does this regularly. She is not helpless. She is perfectly capable to live her secluded life in the sleepy, colorless little town. Still, a group of friends were here for her. Still books to be read. And the son that should call and find out how is she doing. Or to step in after work for a conversation and a glass of wine.

Prostrate on the floor, in her living room, waiting for the son to come. She cannot answer the phone: too far away. Not able to move, her alien leg obscenely displaced and giving her pain.

"It is autumn and the leaves are falling. There were no leaves in my other house where I lived. No tall trees. Only bushes, some flowers, pachysandra and ivy. I wish I could move and see the trees, the leaves and the blue of the sky. But I cannot move. What has happened to me?" The light is disappearing, the darkness is slowly creeping into the house, through the high windows and the dormers, sneaking in and invading the house like a burglar. Slowly, continuously, persistently.

She would like to light a candle. Lighting candles was something mother would do after remembering bad things that happened to her and made her angry. To somehow extinguish or to compensate for her anger, she would light candles and try to get rid of bad thoughts and occasional rages. Thinking of people

97

that were gone or were still alive, capable of hurting her and making her suffer. And making her angry. The darkness is penetrating and she cannot reach the light, cannot light candles. Is he going to call? Is her only son coming to the door to save her? There was no ringing of the telephone. Silence, total silence mixed with darkness. The silence is walking in: no pity, no exceptions. It is the night coming, but in the morning there will be light.

The pain.

The falling into the darkness as if the ocean waves are coming into the house taking over the furniture, the walls, the unlighted candles dragging her into the deep where there is no light. Deep down , there will be no light. Ever. Can she breathe? She is not breathing, there is no oxygen there. She is not a whale that can come to the surface, take the oxygen and dive again and do it again and again and again.

She cannot do it. She is sinking and has no voice. Not able to swim since the leg that lays immobile in a strange position, cannot swim. Is it over?

Daylight is coming and she thinks that her leg is becoming hers again. It is protesting, wishing to move, wishing to let her know. She feels the pain again, but it is distant like a thundering in the distance, so far away, getting farther and farther.

Sinking farther and not caring any more.

There are clouds, and the trees are moving as if wanting to come close to her. Why are the trees moving? They are green and beautiful and the fall is not touching them. A cloud whispers gently and the sun all of sudden is peeking through, giving her warmth. She does not want to think. Slowly, gently, she is freeing herself of her sick leg. Like a ballerina she stands on point and it all seems so easy. She is light, she is becoming colors: green, yellow, grey. Why grey? It should not be grey, but it is. Grey.

The day is coming on. It is pleasant, not cold. Nice and a warm day, for change. Her son comes to the house and rings the door bell. Then takes his keys and enters his mother's house wondering where she could be.

"Mom," he calls and looks around. He sees her on the floor, not moving, not answering the call. He comes closer and frightened, calls out loud.

"Mother, mother, are you all right?"

Memory

The last time we were together was at the seminar in the City. I am back here again and I am all alone. You are long gone. Even when you left, you told me that you would always love me. But I wonder if, in your memories, you remember to love me sometime.

I miss you too much. You were a stranger who attached yourself to me, and then vanished out of my life forever. You took with you a part of my life: some of the woven fabric of my life has been torn away and has disappeared. I feel denuded and vulnerable.

When I talk to other people about you, I often repeat phrases that are easily understood: You were possessive, you were unreasonable, you were given to easy anger bordering on violence. But the simple truth is that I lost something that I held so dear and my healing process is lengthy and poor.

I miss you terribly. All that is left of you for me are a few bittersweet memories that I keep inside. They surface at times like this, and make me sad and unable to function. I imagine things as they might have been: quite different from what perhaps some angry gods have wished upon us. I grieve for what we may have had, but did not. The snowflakes are falling this March. And instead of having heather and daffodils, I am left with the dark gray skies that take my energy away. Nature feels dead, and, thinking of you, so do I.

Part IV: Norma

Traveling Alone

"You only live twice or so it seems,
Once for yourself and once for your dreams…"
Her dream was to return to a place that time ago for her was home.

How deep were the roots? She herself had difficulty deciding. And so it seems that everyone has to have a spot in the universe. A stable, firm spot, like the one Archimedes was looking for, but for which he didn't have enough time to finish – never had time enough to find the stable point from which to be able to move the world.

As for her, she spent her life moving from one place to another like any displaced person might do.

The displacement is not always forced upon the person. It is not always unpleasant, hard to take, brutal. There are displacements done for reasons sometimes not totally clear: the weather, geography, meeting with friends, coworkers, relatives. Or from intellectual or emotional curiosity.

And so it went that Norma, Ms. Norma, Madame Norma, living in an old house in the New Jersey suburbs, decided to visit the island on the Lagoon. The "sun island," the "gold island" with its surroundings where she had spent many summers in her younger days and at that dime considered it a home.

Do people still take leisurely walks along the Adriatic seashore, the beach, the marinas, arm in arm, hand in hand? People of different ages, different physiognomies, sometimes different nationalities? Where big stones are washed by the sea and women and men are eagle-spread on them under the sun, immobile, sometimes asleep, absorbing the sun rays, getting sunburned -- brown, dark brown.

The waters change color as the sun changes its face. The waters of the Adriatic, blue, transparent, joyful, like a young child having fun. Fun and games. But at other times the sea is restless. Its color the color of mud, moody, threatening, unfriendly.

So many faces turned to the Island's shore. Many faces of seasons: spring, summer, fall.

And then winter.

Norma wonders sometimes: where is home? Perhaps the old house in the suburbs, where she has lived the longest, is her home. But are these her roots? Hardly. Does everyone have to have roots? Hardly.

Norma feels a necessity to go. It is a compulsion that she does not quite understand. It would be a great challenge. She would be traveling alone.

It is difficult to imagine: the living in fear of wars, the terror, and the hurricanes that God sends us every so often. Perhaps to punish us or perhaps just as a warning sign, asking us to behave.

And at the same time we move around, fearless, (is it fearless?), invading other cultures and being invaded by others.

Norma thinks that she still feels courageous, can do courageous deeds. Travel alone through the world where danger lurks in every corner, the devil grinning at you mischievously.

"You only live twice."

And so it happened that Norma, Ms. Norma, Madame Norma who lives in an old house in American Suburbia boarded an Alitalia plane to go to the island in the lagoon.

"The day of my departure is getting closer and I am experiencing a sense of wonder. It is a sense of an unknown, foreign and unreal. "Home" is more of a state of mind, a state

of my own fabrication. It is fabricated by me not knowing why, how and where I am going. To go after so many years to see a space and to choose. To choose what?

How hard is when one has imagination.

I am afraid. I do not want to move. I am afraid of the unknown that I may face by myself, getting lost in the reality of the unknown, and not able to reemerge anymore.

The airplane tickets are here, the packed suitcase is here. They are very real physical objects that would conduct me into the world, which seems so unreal to me right now. The unknown, the foreign, the alien. Perhaps it is all just the anxiety of departure, what the Germans used to call a "rise fiber." The fever of traveling. Is the island in the lagoon still there waiting for me, greeting me with the same sunny face of past years? Am I immersing myself into the unknown, where I will get lost and no one will notice?

I am looking forward to seeing my distant cousin whom I remember as practical and, as a matter of fact, pleasant and conventional. Or will I be pushed aside and left to my own remembrances, alien to the place where those remembrances were borne?

Would it be better not to search any more? Less vulnerable for our bodies and souls?

I do not know.

The airplane ticket is a complicated piece of paper (paper, card board, something else?) It does not say much. It is only a copy of an electronic device, which is held at the ticket counter at the airport, and it makes me feel ancient and dispossessed.

However, I am going. And when the mental fog will disappear, I am expected to see the same buildings, old and or restructured, and the same old churches from the fourth century will still be there.

And the Adriatic still moving along with breezes and the seminude bodies on its banks, worshipping the sun.

Norma is ready to go, to board the plane at Newark Liberty airport. Ready to go.

Long lines of travelers, some with rucksacks on their backs, regular travel packs, small valises. She takes off her shoes and steps into the glass box, her artificial knee screaming aloud for all to hear. She is moved out of the glass box into another contraption and taken aside. Everyone is looking at her suspiciously. Her shoes and her bag are on the moving conveyor belt.

She keeps repeating, "I have an artificial knee," but nobody is listening. Taking her aside, a woman gently and politely tells her to spread her arms laterally and goes over her arms, her legs, and her body with an electronic wand.

Her left knee screams again when the woman passes her gadget over it.

"I have an artificial knee," she repeats again, when the woman, satisfied, is letting her go. She grabs her shoes and her bag and limps into the Alitalia gate area, waiting to eventually board the plane.

She finds a small spot on a bench and sits there, unable to read a newspaper, unable to have a sandwich or a cup of coffee. This is what she used to have when traveling with family or friends or a group of tourists.

Nothing seems real.

What is she doing here, waiting patiently, removing her shoes, stepping into a claustrophobic cabin, repeating the phrase:

"My artificial knee."

The world is such today.

Hopefully, everyone will soon be boarding. She will find her seat. She will sit down among strangers, possibly surrounded by bodies if her seat is not on the aisle.

She wishes to be on the aisle. It makes her feel free to move. Free to stand up, to stretch and not to annoy her seat neighbor. She doesn't wish to watch through the window of the plane. Only when the plane gets close to the island on the lagoon will she look at the water to see it from above. Many times before, she would look at the mountains, the Apennines; look at the mountain peaks, some bare, some covered with perpetual snow. Appearing so close you could touch them and fee the silence they offer as a gift or as a prayer. So vast and so peaceful. So timeless that she had felt in other times the urge, the invitation, to step outside and lie down in all that silence.

But it is different now: the silence is not for her to share. Only the anticipation of the uneventful flight.

Alone, squeezed between strangers, unable to move properly, feeling stupid. Her neck is hurting her and her knee is making her know that it is not pleased with her traveling experience. Norma thinks how she would look if she puts her special collar around her neck and knows that no one will care what she is doing. Or how she looks. The strangers are all in their own world, their own worries, and their own concerns. All strangers to each other, silent, not trusting, not friendly, not sharing.

The world of today. Where humanity is collected in one large amorphous globe of bodies, breaths and possible tears.

Norma is thinking that if she had her family, her friends, her fellow churchgoers with her, she would be less aware of all this. Some positive energy would have encircled her and she would have been able to maybe read a book and ignore the noises.

She has no one with her. She thinks how we lose each other, one by one, into the mud of the past, present and the "plus quam perfectum."

All is unreal and yet so palpable, so unpleasantly physical.

She is traveling alone.

"We only live twice, or so it seems, one life for ourselves and one for our dreams."

Is is not an impulse; it is an obsession, a compulsion. No wonder it all looks unreal to her. Alone, she is traveling toward an island in the lagoon. Perhaps for the last time and perhaps not. With her stiff neck and her artificial knee. Not so bad.

It is cold in her place on the lagoon. The end of October and the weather is becoming unfriendly. Norma tries to get warm by putting the heat on. The place is empty with no sense of energy. After her long absence, the place does not recognize her.

Norma thinks that because of the time difference between here and America, and because time is relative, capriciously multidimensional, while her body is made of matter, thickness with no transparency, the cold of the place is more pronounced.

Her face is cold, her ears ache and her head seems to have grown large and slightly stiff. How do we cross oceans, time barriers, cultures, with a sense of belonging or not, without becoming confused, slow thinking, sleepy, cold. Abandoned by the universe. Abandoned by the everyday routine in search of past times, past memories, which become myths over the years and may lose the reality that created them.

Tired, headachy from the trip, she walks out to the streets and to the boat basin that is visible from her window.

The water always calms her down. In spite of her weakness, the confusion that she feels from the hangover of the tip, there is something comfortable and reassuring in the streets filled with people. Young and old, men and women, and the store windows full of merchandise and lights.

She walks by herself, slowly, avoiding meeting anyone. The main street has her favorite bookstore, her favorite café. She will start tomorrow. In spite of the cold, in spite of the tiredness that makes her vulnerable, somewhere within her resides a sense of goodness, a sense of peace.

The next day it is not so cold. She puts on a relatively heavy jacket and the outdoors seems somehow warm. People walk around: food shopping, window-shopping. Expensive or not, everything belongs to all, to look at and to enjoy. It is beautiful to walk through.

It is the end of the season, October with a touch of the autumn. Sitting in a café, she has a cappuccino and reads a newspaper. She walks by herself and does not feel lonely. Deep down she feels a common connection.

What is it?

Belonging and not belonging.

Walking through the streets, going to the water's edge. In the evening, the sun on the horizon will soon disappear, and the night will come. Time to leave the water. Time to have coffee or gelato and then supper.

This is a happy place.

Norma is looking, searching. In all this beauty, the quaintness and light, is there also a sense of worry and a sense of resignation toward the unhealthiness of the world? Because our world is not healthy. Do we still have the capacity to adjust?

Do people still love each other? Men, women, children looking at the sunset or the sunrise, dreaming of togetherness, of distant shores, the changing colors. The melody of creation.

Again and again, she looks from her window onto the narrow port, full of small and medium-sized boats. Is there a couple on one of them that is setting sail onto the wide distance, just to taste the day, to taste today? Are they going to sail into tomorrow? Perhaps it is "arrivederci" till the next adventure. She thinks that her imagination is running away from her. She does not know what is in people's hearts or heads.

The clouds are collecting above. It is going to be bad weather again.

Lucy came to visit. Lucy is the daughter of a relative, an elderly aunt now deceased. After her mother's death, Lucy remained close to Norma, staying friends to share friendship and memories, to walk together through the town or visit other places.

Lucy is also an interesting person, very specific and sure about the statements she makes, her knowledge vast and somewhat unusual, as her interests are unusual. She is an animal lover, which makes her collect stray dogs and cats that she cares about and finds shelters for them or families to adopt them. She knows all about different birds and bees, and Norma does not dare to ask about other species like snakes, flies and cockroaches. Lucy would never kill a bird or a bee! She even feeds the pigeons, and everyone complains, but that does not stop her.

Norma has called Lucy to come and visit her on the island. Over the phone they have set a date and Lucy had asked the usual question:

"How are you doing?" (She has not seen her for some time.)

"I am good, thank you, but I am aging," Norma answers.

Lucy's answer is matter of fact:

"These days we humans can live to be one hundred and twenty-five."

"How do you think that this may be true?" Norma asks.

"These are the statistics," Lucy answers. "The present young generation should last to one hundred twenty-five. So your generation may still last up to ninety."

"Is that a consoling fact or something to worry about?" Norma thought. "Is this too long to live and to remember? I am going to find out a little more about it when I see her. Soon."

It is October and by the evening it gets cold. Not overly cold but cold. Norma had walked all afternoon. To the bookstore, for the newspapers. She bought a few little gifts for friends and family. Inexpensive ones. Times are hard and one should be frugal. The place is heated for the evening and the night, and it is comfortable. She steps out on the balcony and watches the narrow port. Lights are shimmering on the water. The boats are all in a line, next to each other, small, medium and some fairly large. The masts are sticking high, like a forest with trees, tall and elegant, pointing to the heaven. On the sidewalk next to the port, a man on a bicycle rides by. A few people walk by, going somewhere. It is quiet: the summer season has ended. Only on the weekend do folks still come to walk the narrow streets, visit the churches, and look at the shops.

But even on quiet nights one knows that the place is alive. One knows that the cafés, the small restaurants and the large ones will open up tomorrow. And in the early hours, the bakery shop will be open with the smell of baked bread filling the street.

How long with this last? She thinks. For a long time. She hopes that it is forever.

Lucy comes to spend the day with her on the island and somehow brings reality into Norma's musings. She tells her about her health problems, the surgery she has to have on her left eye because of the dark spot on her vitreous. It is not moaning or whining but said as a matter of fact, so they make plans for the day.

Norma asks Lucy the question she definitely wanted Lucy to clarify, "Why do you think we humans should live to be one hundred twenty-five years old?"

"Our bones are matured and totally developed by the age of twenty five," Lucy says. "No more developing after that. And we should last five times that number. Which then brings us to one hundred twenty-five."

Norma did not ask where and how these statistics were collected. Lucy did add that we do not live healthy lives; therefore this age may not be achieved by all.

"We smoke, we drink excessively and," she adds, "we eat meat."

"Meat is just a cadaver," Lucy says. (Was it Seneca, a Roman philosopher, who said he did not want a cadaver on his table?)

A vegan, Lucy does not eat meat. Or fish. Or prosciutto.

They go to a restaurant through the narrow, winding streets of the old city. It is outdoors but surrounded by old buildings, houses that may not be demolished. So many old houses. It is so pleasant and intimate to sit outdoors and be served lunch. It is like being in one's own little fiefdom.

The day is warm, no need for a sweater or a jacket. Hopefully, it will continue like that till the day she returns to New Jersey.

They take a trip by ferry boat through the lagoon that leads them to a silent island, where there are only churches, religious houses, flowers, trees and birds. In the shallow water, small fish jump in and out and the crabs move sideways on the wet sand.

Herons stand in the shallow water, immobile, as if meditating, their necks long and curved, and the dark cormorants are also walking through the shallows.

The lagoon is full of birds. Seagulls above, so many of them. Big, with large wings spread widely, gliding through the air. Lucy tells her that the seagulls are rapacious and go not only after fish, but also after the small birds that collect in groups at the time of going south. The seagulls. Beautiful and rapacious.

The air is so pure.

At times, Norma feels again as if she is losing herself in the present, the past being something that she just invented in moments of poetic license. Or in moments when she remembers clearly and precisely how it used to be, once upon a time. (Probably both may be true.)

The seagulls on the lagoon and on the island are big. The seagulls back home are small in comparison. Less white, less large, probably less rapacious. The pigeons are the same everywhere, aggressive, fresh, looking for any kind of food, mostly fed by persons who bring them breadcrumbs. Then they conglomerate, attack the crumbs and chase each other for wanting more. Sometimes they fly to the table where one eats, especially when there are sweets. They arrogantly descend, flap their wings and want part of the cake.

How interesting to watch the seagulls and the pigeons. Lucy loves them both. She is the one who takes pieces of bread from the table and feeds them to the pigeons when no one is watching.

She will return again to take another outing with Norma to the surrounding countryside. It feels to Norma as if Lucy has always been there and never left, regardless of distance or time.

It was pleasant. They did not hide from the sun. Norma took Lucy to the train station and returned to the house. Relaxed and happy.

It is five o'clock and daylight savings time has taken effect. The last weekend of October. I am listening to the bells from the old fourth century church, the one in the center of the town very close to me. It is possible that the bells are not the ones that were ringing years back. Then, a man pulled the ropes tied to the bells, pulled them rhythmically and persistently to make them ring. The "angelus," the calling of members for prayers and meditation.

I suspect that now it is done by some remote control in the bell tower, the result of the high technology of our century. All the same, it is so beautifully inspiring to listen to the sounds of the invisible bells in the late afternoons. Then some of us will descend to the piazza to have coffee, and some of us will go to the fourth century old church to pray. High ceilings, old walls showing humidity stains, and the mosaic floor covered by a red carpet to save it from being worn out.

(In silence and alone I am savoring the moment.)

Norma still has to see her cousin Genia who lives in the city, about an hour away from the island. The city where Norma was born, and which she left with her family, a long time ago.

Her cousin is expecting her. She wants to take Norma to the museum that was once the home of an old family long gone, but their home is still there and can be seen by the public only at certain hours of the day. Norma is intrigued by this home on a busy street, almost invisible among the other buildings. While apparently nondescript, its walls hold a history of the city, along with a history of an old family long gone. The importance of memories, the importance of knowing and of seeing.

But she is tired today and does not wish to drive into the city by herself, alone. So she decides to phone her cousin, and postpone the visit to the museum, as well as lunch and a visit with some friends she would like to see again. She is sorry about this and reprimands herself for her weakness, physical and mental, for missing a day of beauty, togetherness, friendship.

"Do not be so hard on yourself," she thinks. "No need to be a hero. You are not a hero. Just a tired person who does not wish to drive."

She calls her cousin to reschedule the get-together.

Her cousin is positive, so supportive in her understanding of her. It seems as if they had left each other only very recently. She promptly reschedules another meeting in two days. They will see each other with the rest of the family and friends and, at that time, will visit the city and possibly the museum.

It sounds so beautiful.

She is going to rest and get strong. She will drive into the city and visit the people she loves. She prepares herself for a long rest, a full night's sleep. "To sleep, perchance to dream." Unlike Hamlet, Norma welcomes her dreams.

Getting up early in the morning and driving away, possibly about an hour of driving. Through the Riviera, high above the Adriatic, then descending into the city and parking the car "sulla riva." That is where I have always parked my car, in other times. I am a little bit anxious: perhaps they have no more parking spots on the marina. Perhaps they have built big garages like the one in New York City on 8th Avenue. I would have to drive through it, looking for parking.

Let's hope there is a spot on the marina.

Lucy complains about traffic, about buildings going up where trees used to be (surprise!). About the city not being clean enough. Lucy is spoiled. Norma will see what Genia thinks.

To Norma, the city is still quaint, with its traffic jams, with people walking haphazardly through the streets making the car drivers angry. There is something entertaining in all that.

Genia and her husband, Gianni, meet her and try to pamper her. "Are you tired?" They ask her and take her arm, thinking that she needs help in walking.

"I do not walk long distances," she tells them. "I have a bad knee."

They take her around, walking slowly, holding her hand or walking "sottobraccio." She lets them do it, but feels slightly embarrassed, a bit like an invalid. Still, it is nice to be taken care of.

Dinner in their home, served in the dining room with guests whom she knows.

In the morning they walk to the gallery, to see an antique show. No museum this time. "Sara' per un 'altra volta."

The building with the gallery in it is on the water, on the pier where big ships used to dock. The water is there and the air is invigorating. She does not experience pollution, although there must be some. It is ubiquitous, she knows. And yet, to her, it feels pure.

The antique show is there every year in the same season. Norma and Genia have promised each other not to buy anything. In the past times, they always bought compulsively: bought beautiful and useless objects. This time they are frugal. No buying. They laugh as they pass by the "temptings" and remind each other of their promise.

She spends two days with them, walking, talking, eating. Then she returns to her place on the island.

Her place at present.

With promises to write to them.

With promises to keep in touch, promises they all intend to keep.

She will remember that at times, it was like walking through a dreamscape, with the reality that at times bounced upon her and would make her surprised. Perhaps frightened a little, as if she did not know why she was there.

Soon, Norma is to return to her old house in the New Jersey suburbs. On the edge of town. The tall trees surround the house and the maple leaves are accumulating on the floor of the veranda and on the table that is out there.

She'll clear the leaves from the table, sit there, read a book or write notes to friends and relatives whom she has left on the lagoon and on the seaside.

"The last hurdle of my "pilgrimage." Packing up my suitcase. Fixing my face so it will look beautiful with all its wrinkles.

Last look, last surprising look about the place that is still standing: the stores, the libraries, and the port. And it all will be there after I have left.

The separation.

The time difference. Time, meaning the distance from one point to another and I am floating in both, sometimes lost and sometimes found. Found myself.

Perhaps all this is not real. Perhaps the reality is just the streets, the traffic, the supermarkets.

It is cold again. As she puts her coat on, she buttons it as if to protect her inner self. She is going back home. The leaving is also home for her. How many homes may one person have? Perhaps everyone should have only one.

"Never mind" she thinks, "I am leaving and I will return. In the end, I like it this way."

It is the wind.

The winter is coming. November. Mornings are dark. So are the evenings. And the wind is blowing, shaking the trees in front of the windows. The sun comes out. But the wind makes her feel cold and unprotected in spite of the sun.

It is time to return. It is all right to return. To stay indoors in winter. To light the lamp and to read. To continue breathing, in, out, in, out, and to wait for spring.

Running away from the wind makes it easier to leave. Leaving, always leaving. But returning also, and, once again, being at home.

Many homes, few homes. Just two homes.

It was cold when I came, and it is cold now that I am leaving. In between, there were beautiful sunny days with no wind and the sea limpid, quiet, pale blue in the distance, a liquid crystal sparkling with colors. And walking without a coat, letting the sun kiss our faces, getting a slight suntan.

So, no complaints. The variables in life we cannot control, but we make them acceptable. And, at times perhaps, also pleasant.

Cold air, deep breathing, inhaling, cleansing our lungs.

It is good.

It is a nice goodbye.

APPENDIX

Page 16, 17 *La Nuestra Señora De Guadalupe*: The Madonna, patron saint of the Spanish people in New Mexico and Arizona.

Page 20- *virgo intacta* – virgin

Page 34 *Partir C'est Mourir Un Peu* by Edmond Haraucourt, 1891.

"To depart is to die a little; To die to what we love; One leaves a little of one's self, In every hour and in every place; And one leaves, and it's a game; And until the final farewell, with one's soul one makes one's mark at each goodbye."

Page 60 *Manana* – tomorrow.

Page 81 *O tempora, o mores:* Oh what a time, oh what customs!

Page 86 *Alti Piani*: Upland Plains.

Page 87 *Cordillera Blanca*: Spanish for "White Range"; is a mountain range in the Ancash Region of Peru.

Page 88 *Cogito Ergo Sum*: "I think, therefore I am." Rene Descartes, French Philosopher (1596-1650).

Page 93 "Ognuno per se stesso e Dio per tutti," Everyone for themselves and God for everyone.

Page 99   *Sic Transit Gloria Mundi*: "Thus the glory of the world passes."

Page 104   *Danse Macabre*: Dance of Death.

Page 109 "You Only Live Twice." Lyrics by Nancy Sinatra, music by John Barry.

Page 116 *Sottobraccio*: arm in arm.

Page 116   *Sarà per un'altra volta*: It will happen another time.

Printed in the United States
136541LV00002B/1/P